JESS KEATING

# BUNBUN & BONBON

## FANCY FRIENDS

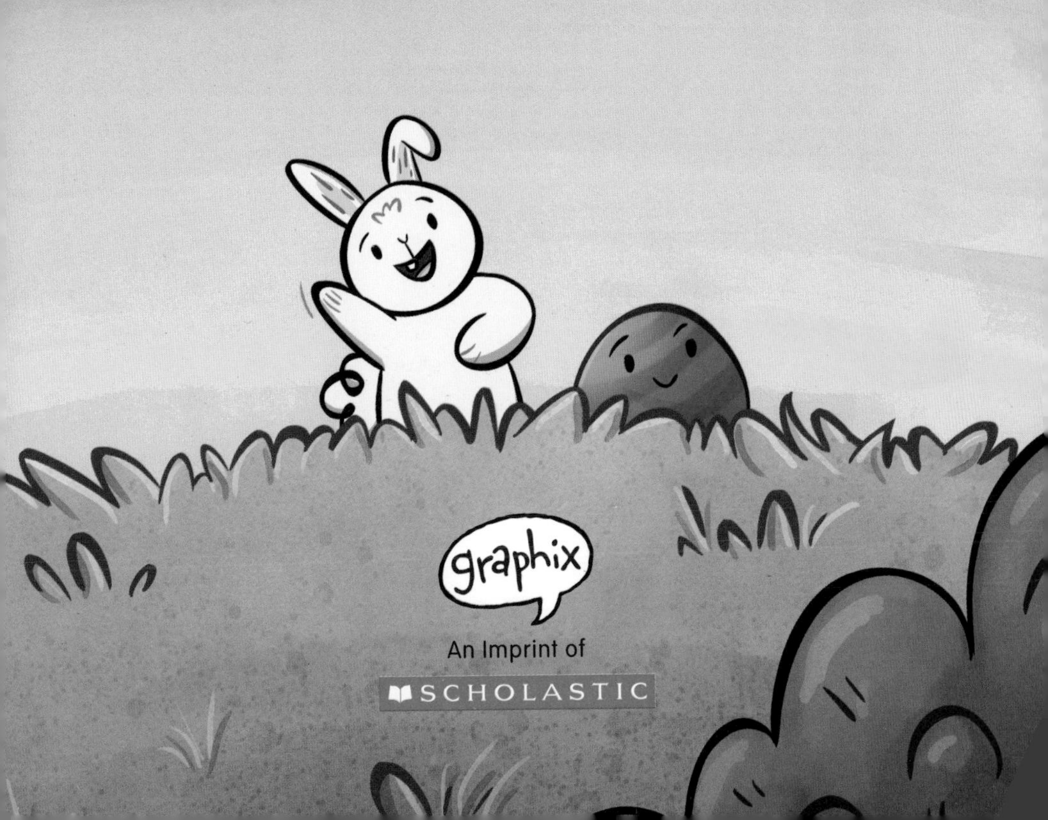

graphix
An Imprint of
SCHOLASTIC

To Sayuri & Dav, Ken & Jonah —
the fanciest (and loveliest!) of friends.

All rights reserved. Published by Graphix, an imprint of Scholastic Inc.,
*Publishers since 1920.* SCHOLASTIC, GRAPHIX, and associated logos are
trademarks and/or registered trademarks of Scholastic Inc.

The publisher does not have any control over and does not assume any
responsibility for author or third-party websites or their content.

This book is a work of fiction. Names, characters, places, and incidents are either
the product of the  author's imagination or are used fictitiously, and any resemblance
to actual persons, living or dead, business establishments, events, or locales
is entirely coincidental.

Library of Congress Control Number: 2019957360

ISBN 978-1-338-64683-2 (hardcover)
ISBN 978-1-338-64682-5 (paperback)

10 9 8 7 6 5 4 3 2 1          20 21 22 23 24

Printed in China          62
First edition, September 2020
Edited by Ken Geist and Jonah Newman
Book design by Phil Falco and Steve Ponzo
Color assistance: Wes Dzioba
Creative Director: Phil Falco
Publisher: David Saylor

# CONTENTS

**5**

WHEN BUNBUN MET BONBON

**25**

TEAM FANCY!

**35**

A FANCY GARDEN PARTY!

**49**

DONUTS FOR LUNCH!

**57**

BEST FRIENDS FOREVER
AND EVER!

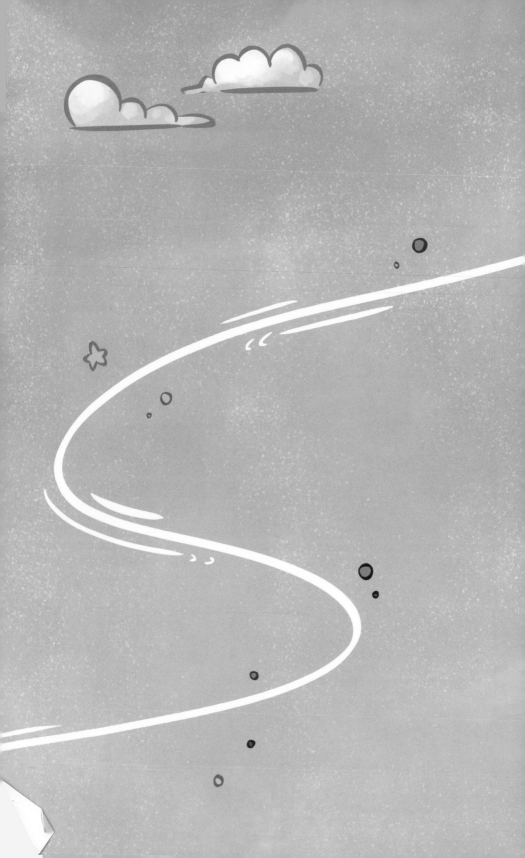

# WHEN BUNBUN
# MET BONBON

**Bunbun** had it all.
A delightful Bunbun nose,
a winning Bunbun smile,
a ridiculously cute
Bunbun tail . . .

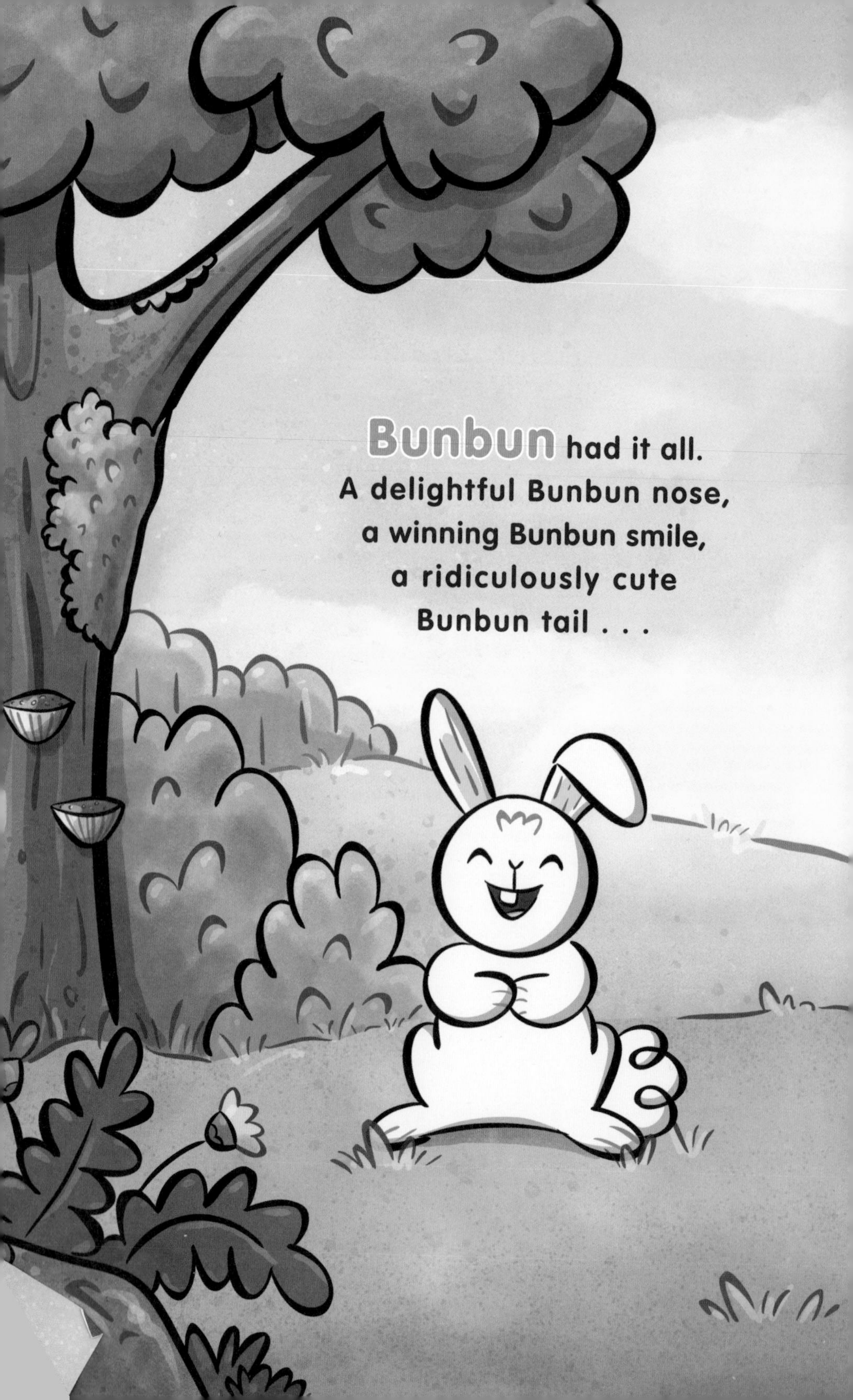

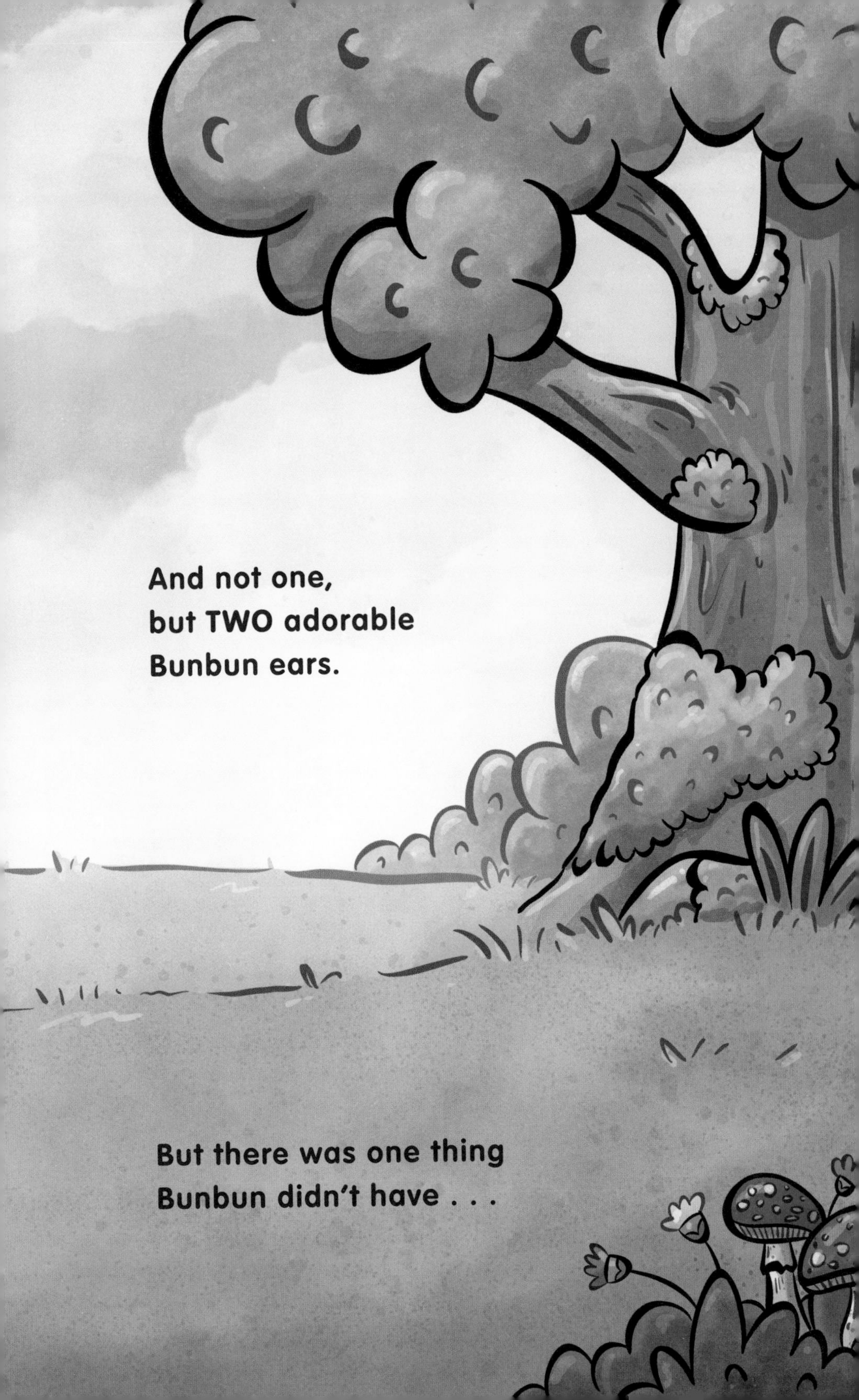

And not one,
but TWO adorable
Bunbun ears.

But there was one thing
Bunbun didn't have . . .

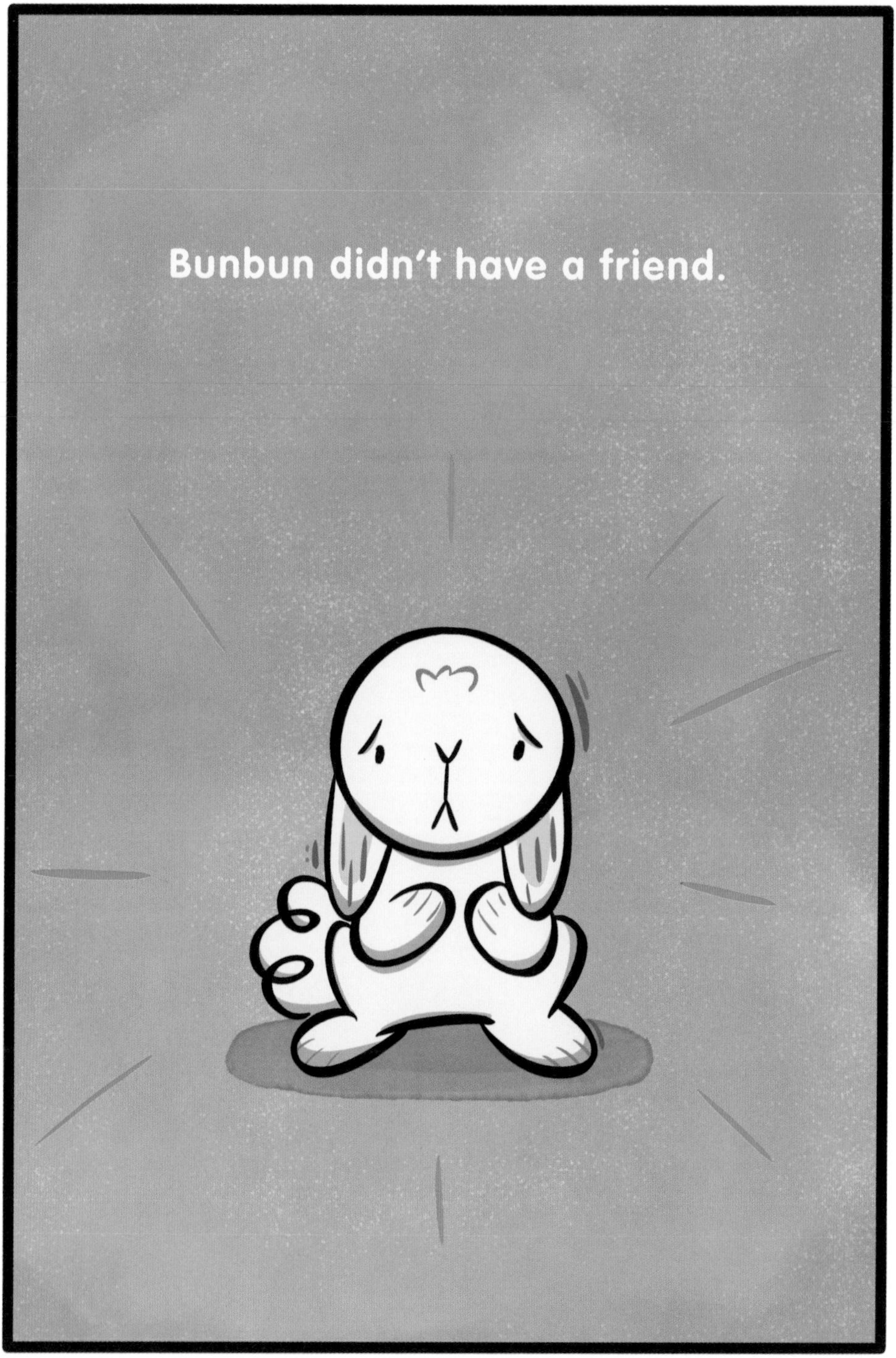
Bunbun didn't have a friend.

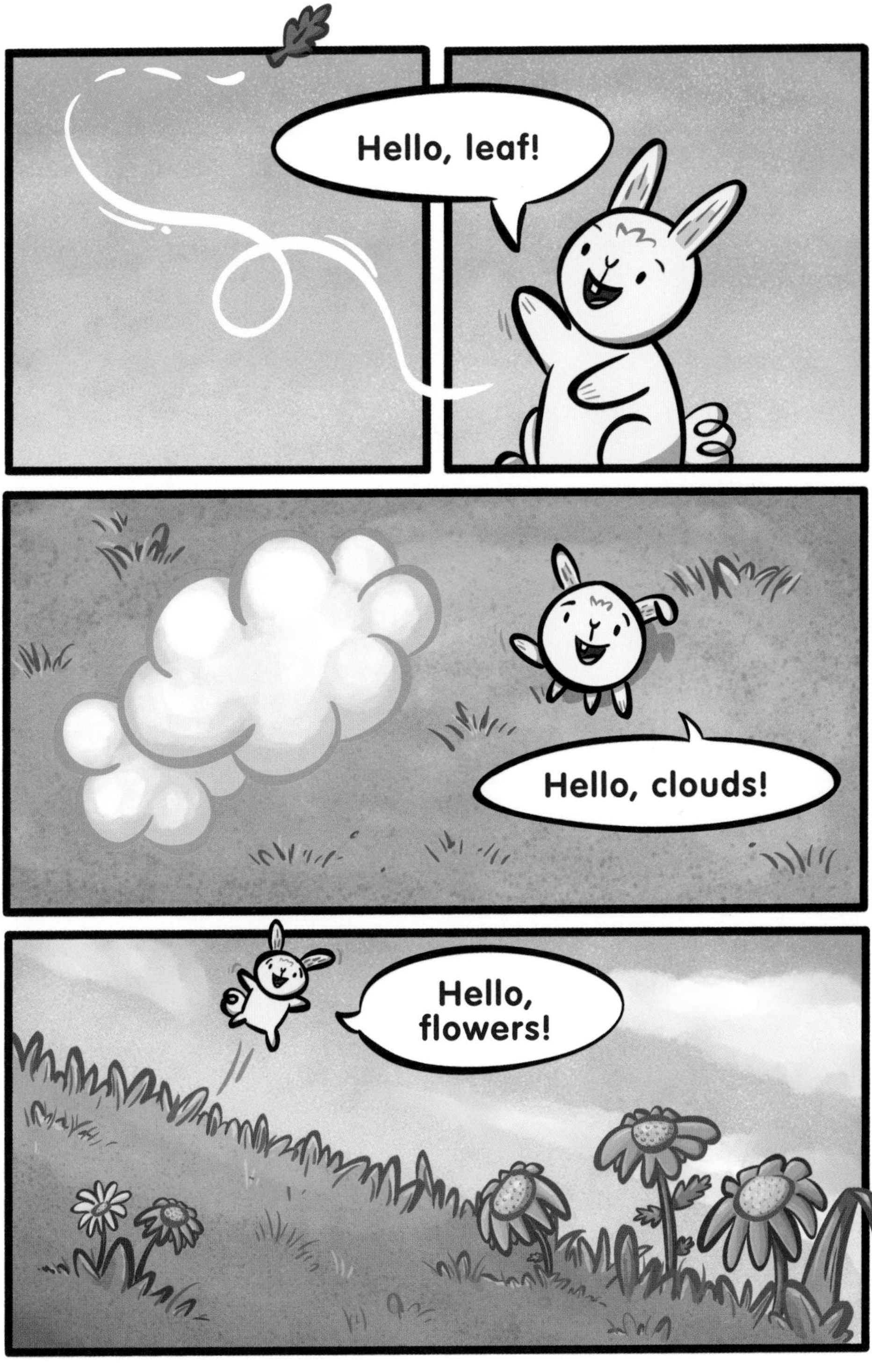
Hello, leaf!
Hello, clouds!
Hello,
flowers!

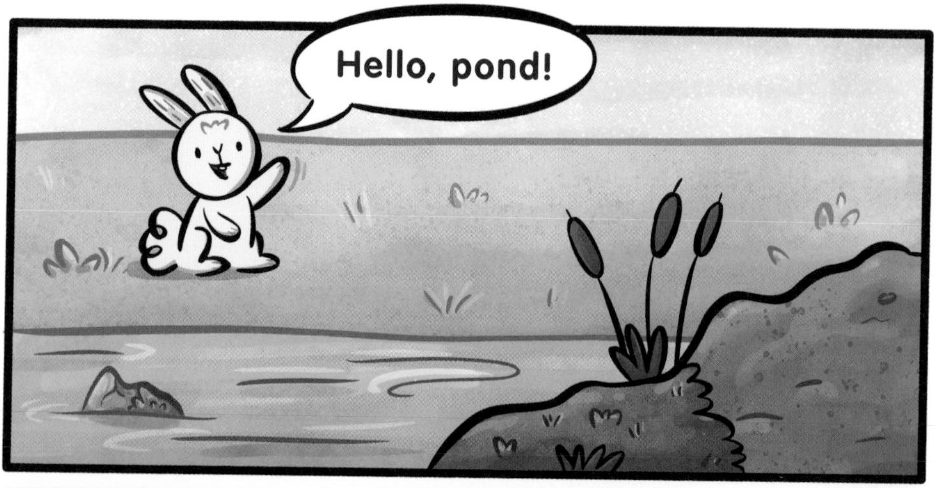
Hello, pond!

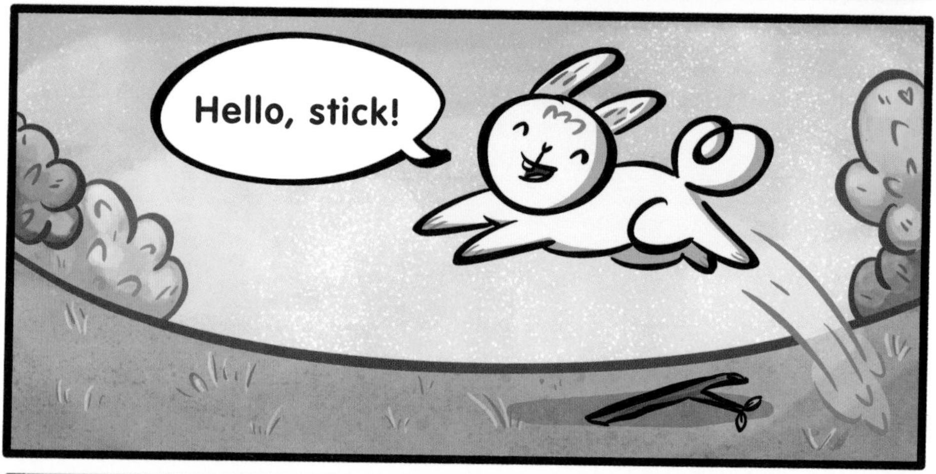
Hello, stick!

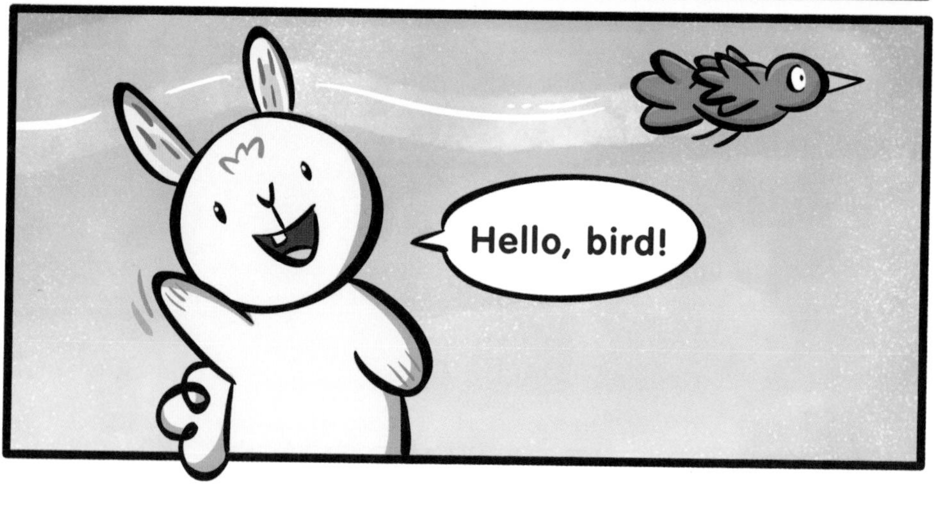
Hello, bird!

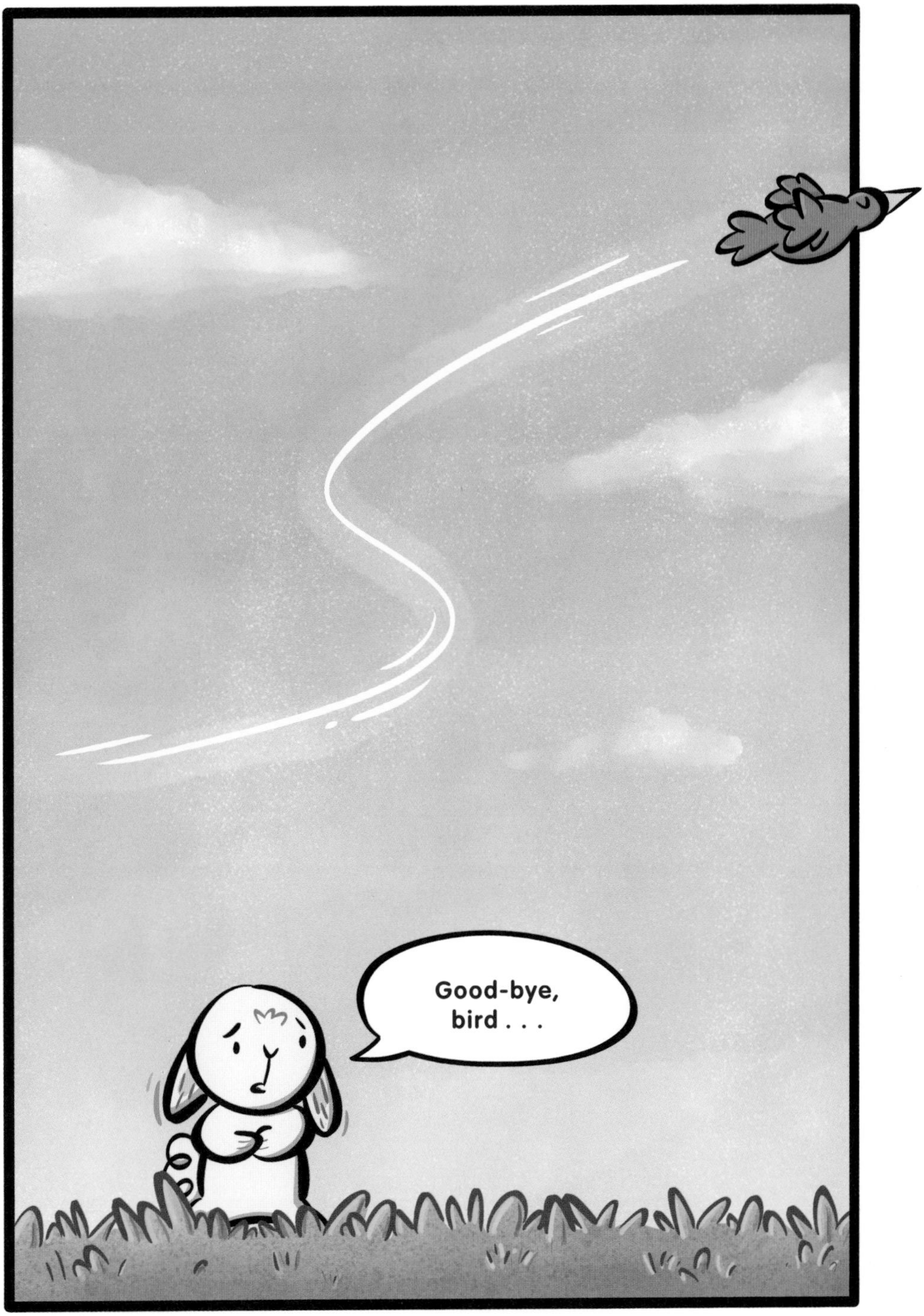
Good-bye, bird . . .

UNTIL ONE DAY . . .

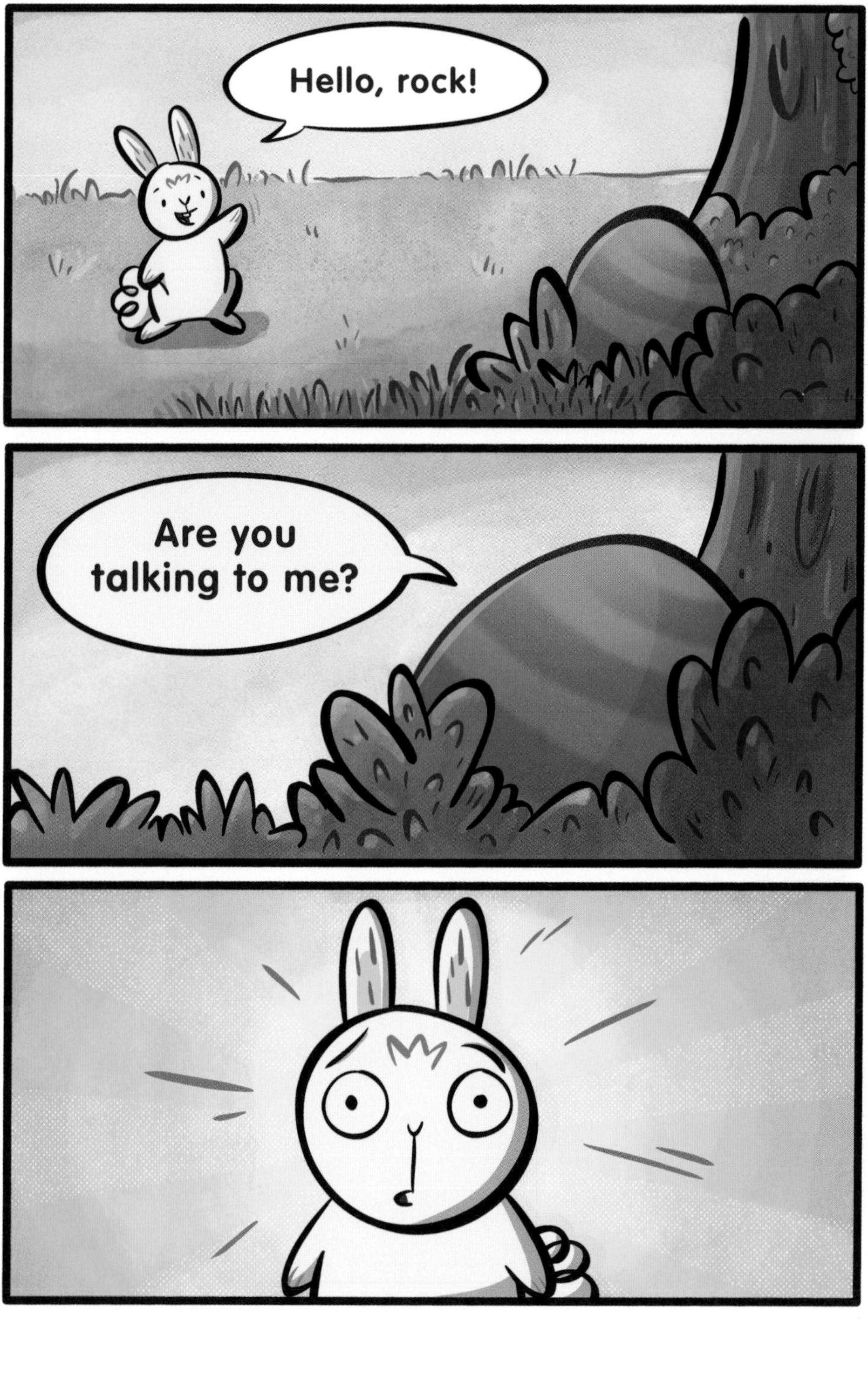

Hello, rock!
Are you talking to me?

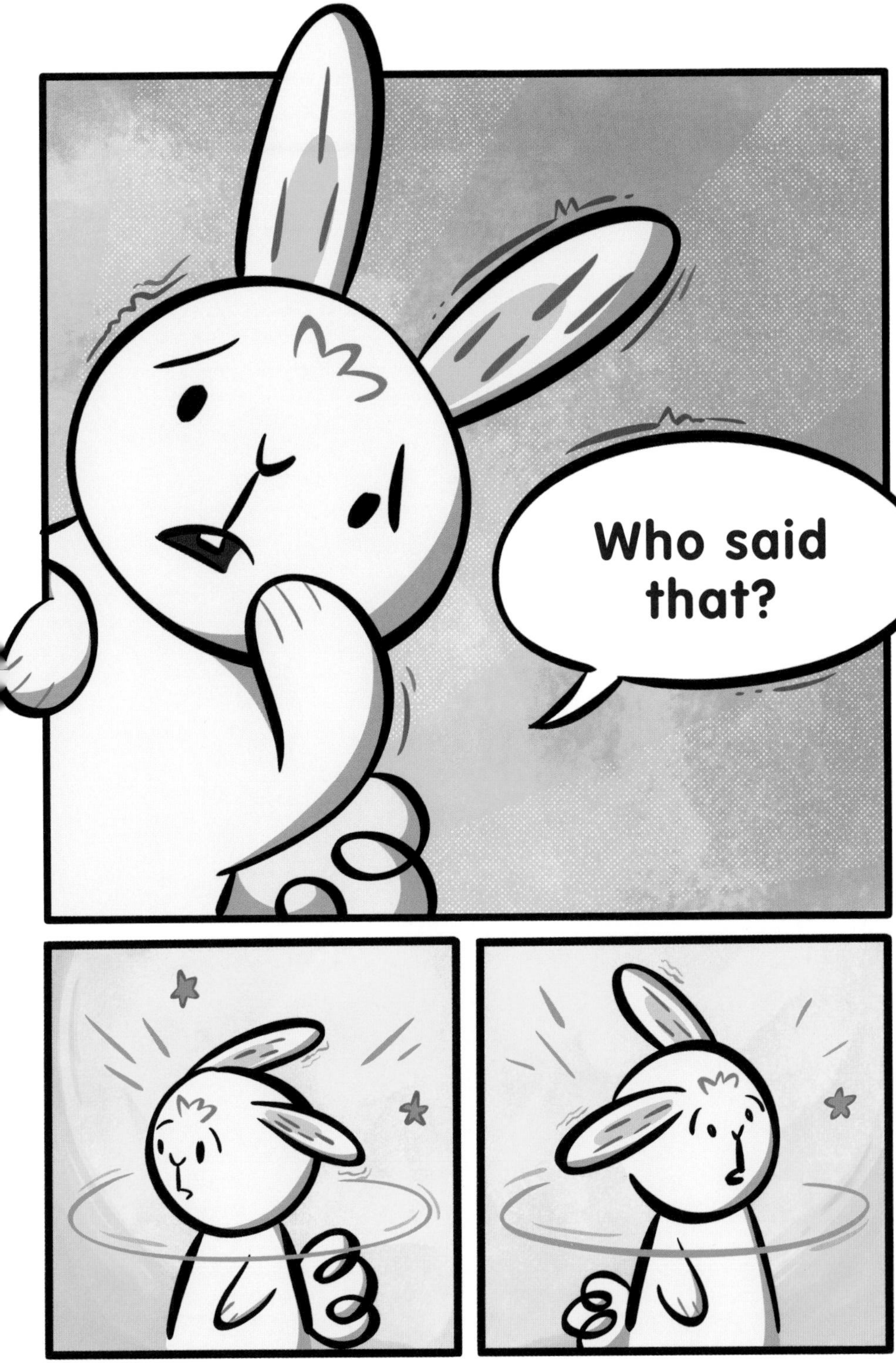
Who said that?

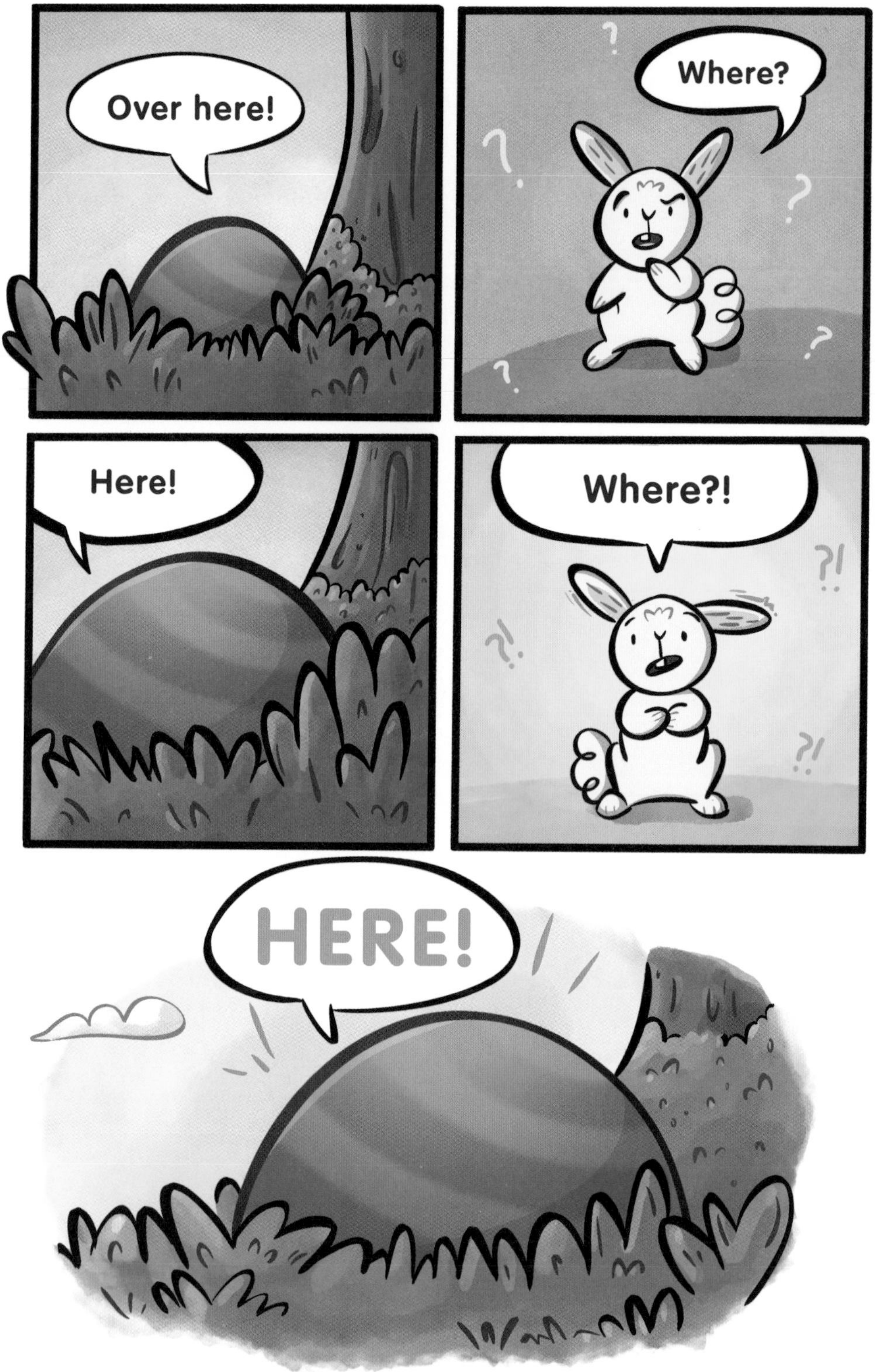
Over here!
Where?
Here!
Where?!
HERE!

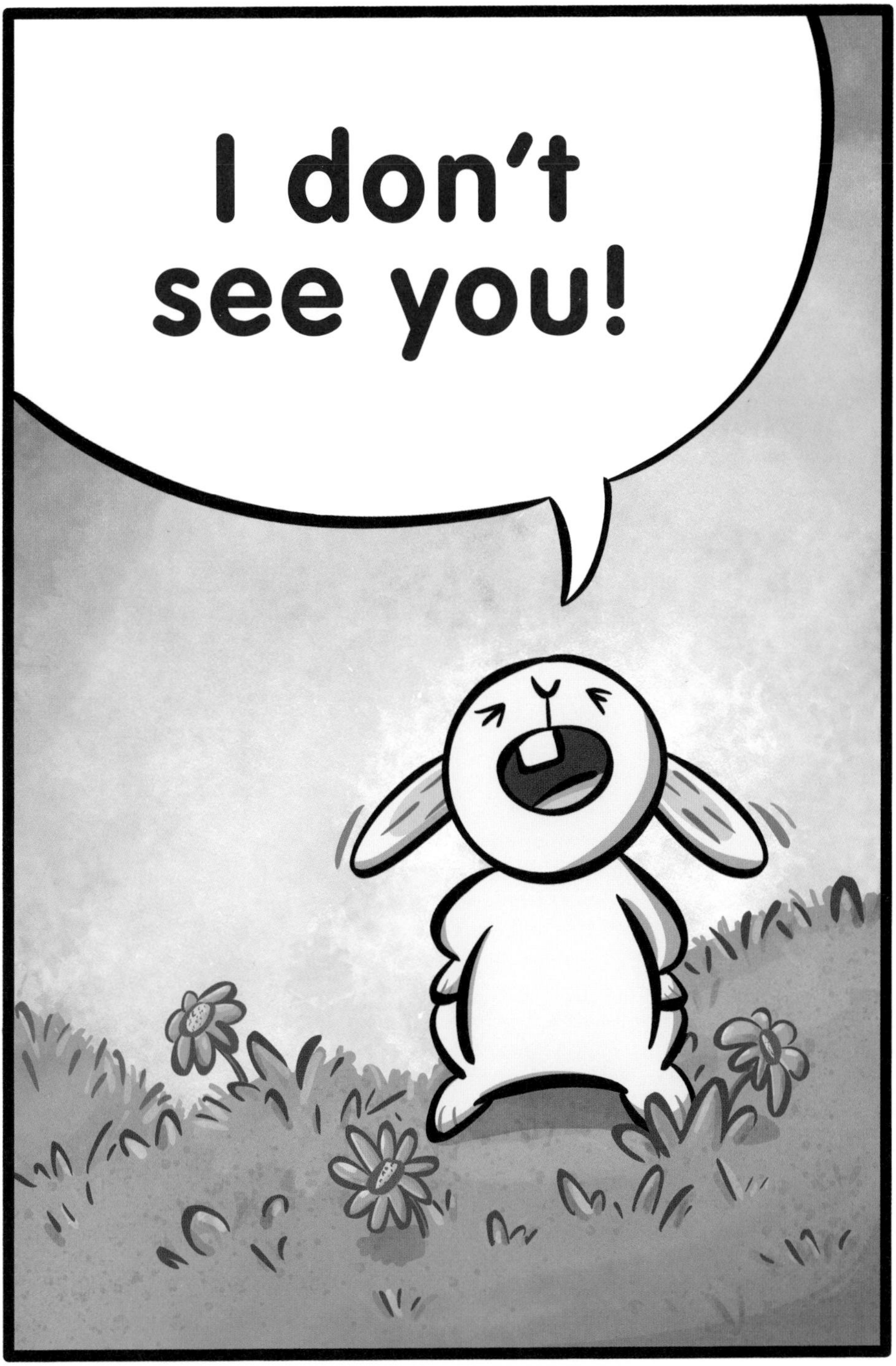
I don't see you!

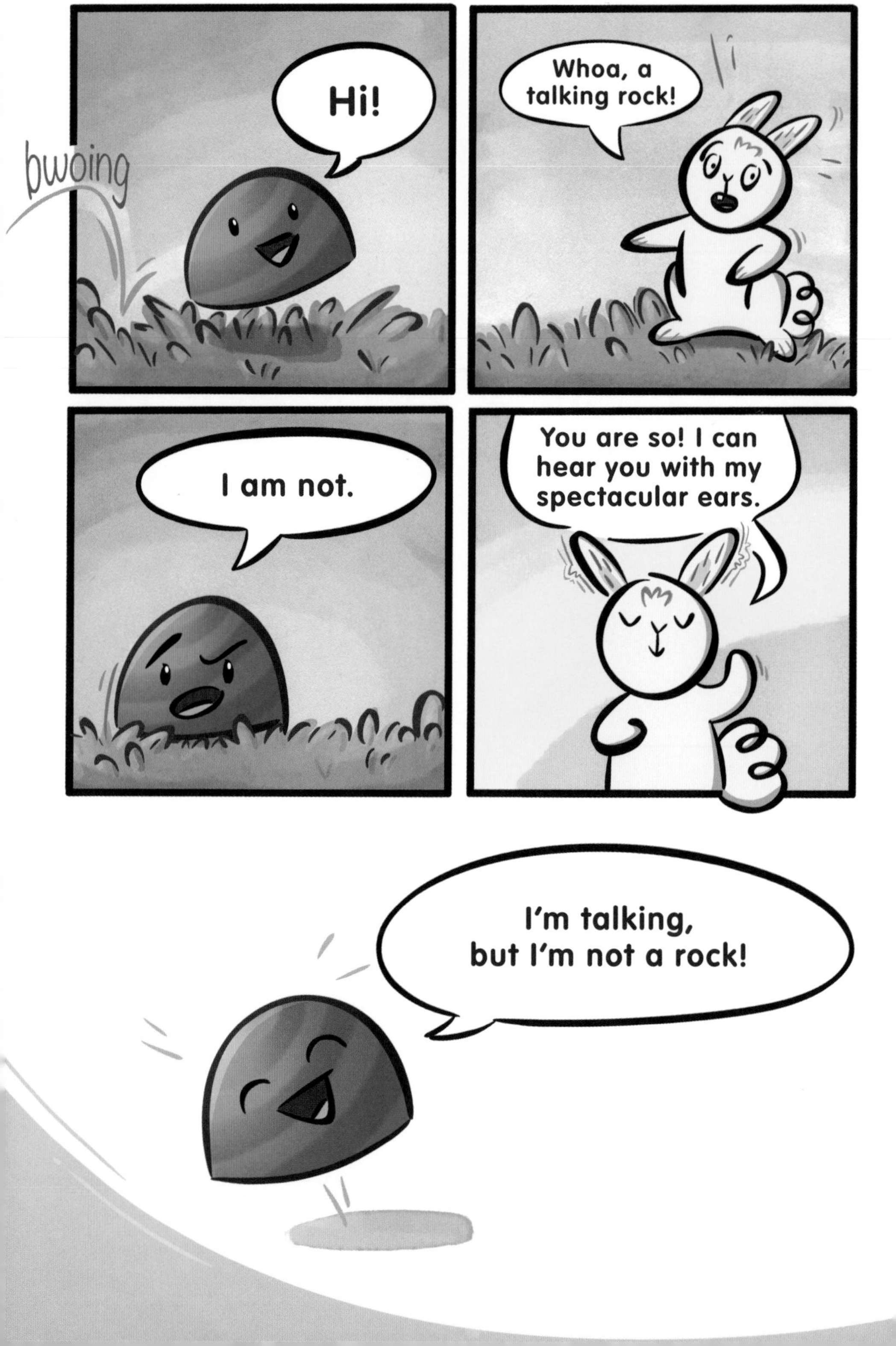
bwoing
Hi!
Whoa, a talking rock!
I am not.
You are so! I can hear you with my spectacular ears.
I'm talking, but I'm not a rock!

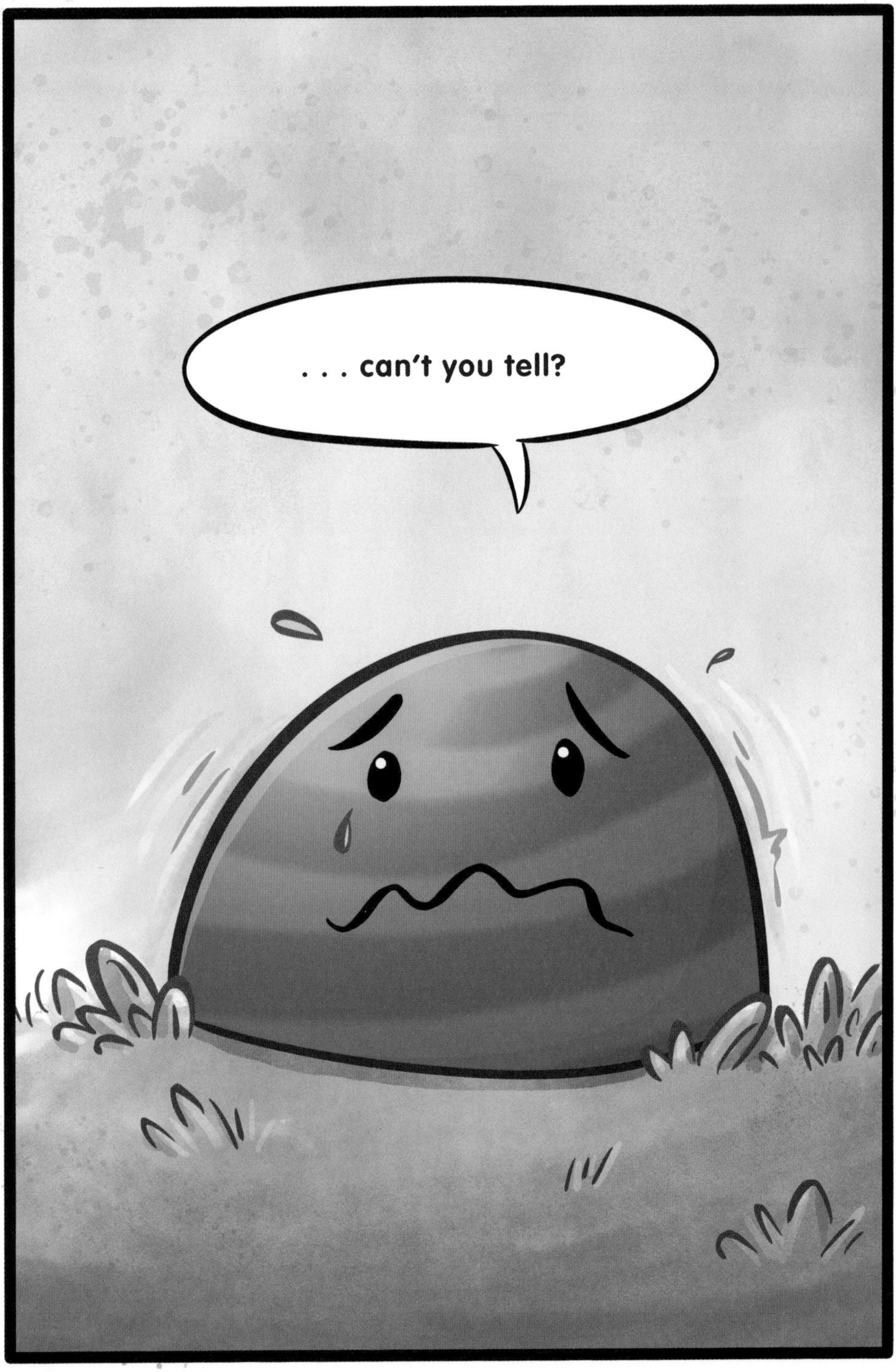
. . . can't you tell?

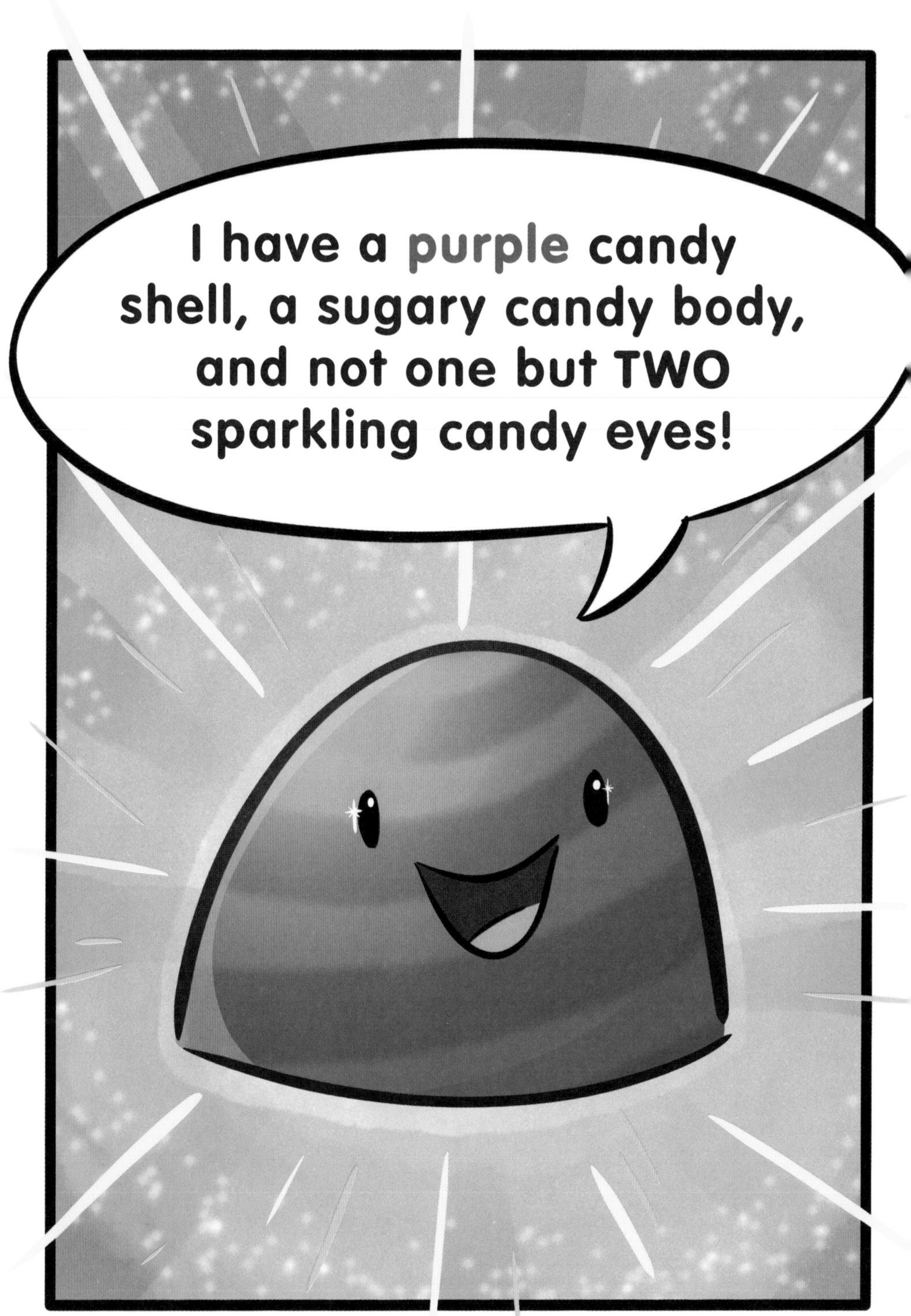
I have a purple candy shell, a sugary candy body, and not one but TWO sparkling candy eyes!

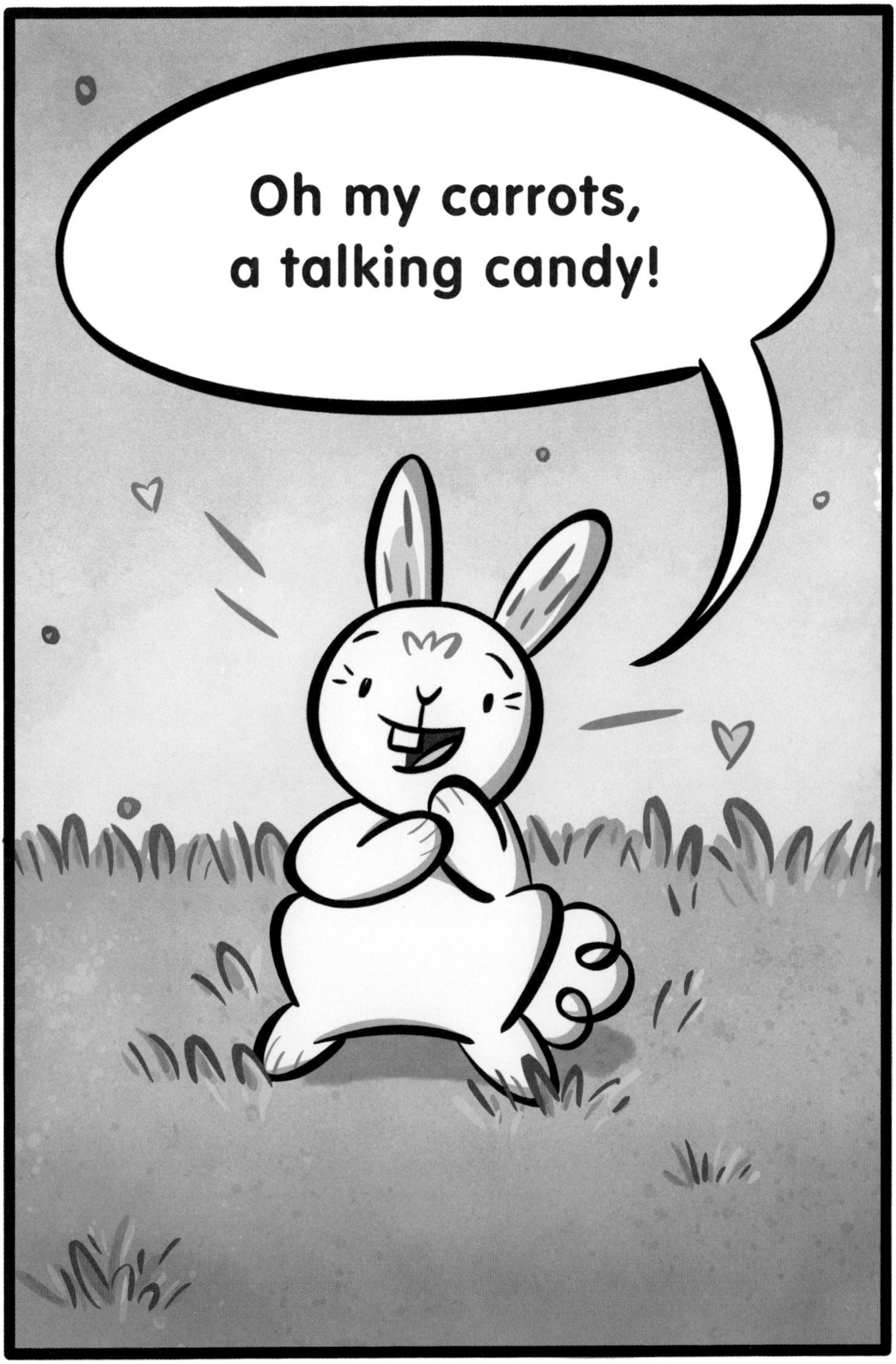
Oh my carrots, a talking candy!

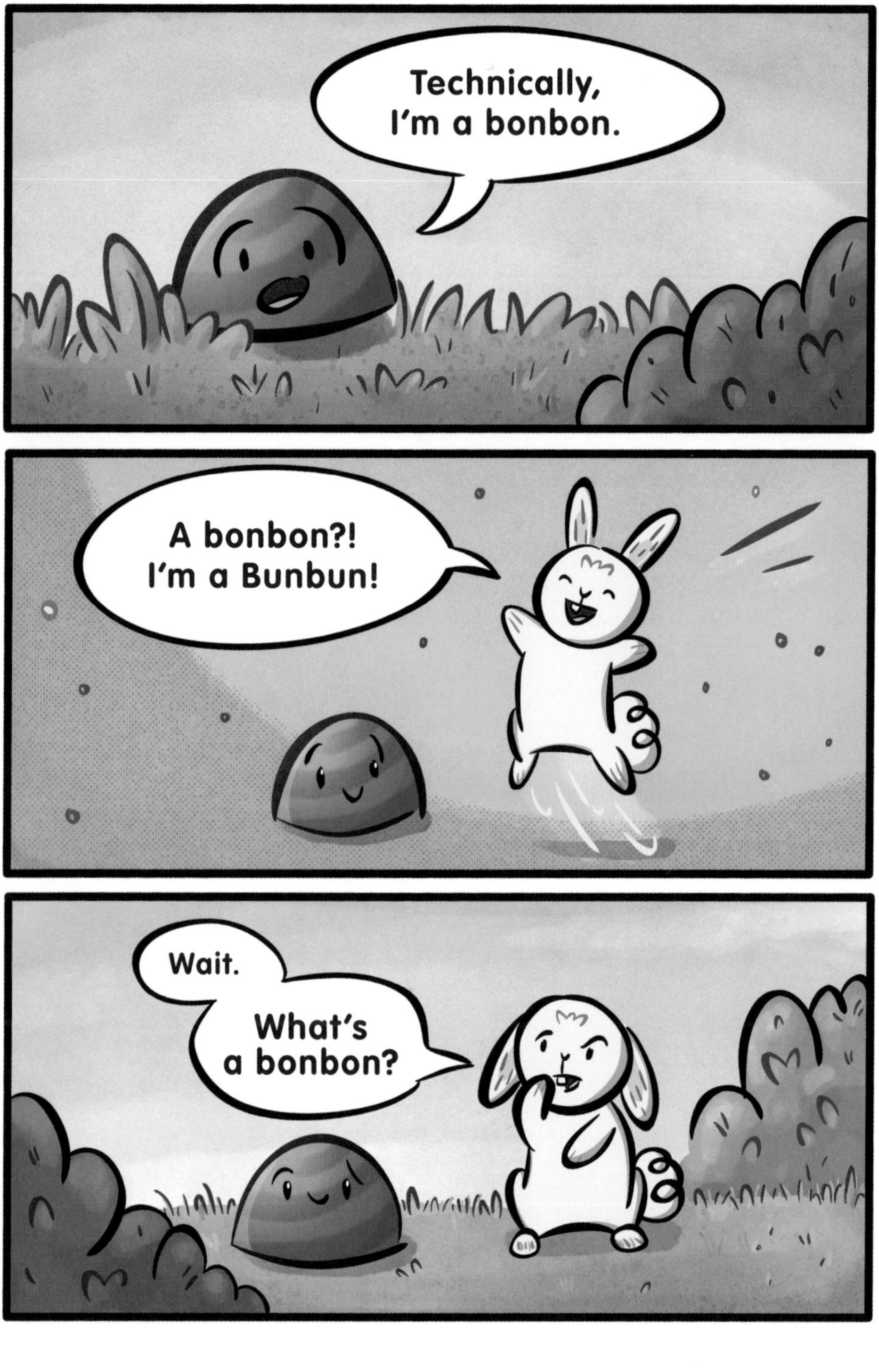
Technically, I'm a bonbon.
A bonbon?! I'm a Bunbun!
Wait.
What's a bonbon?

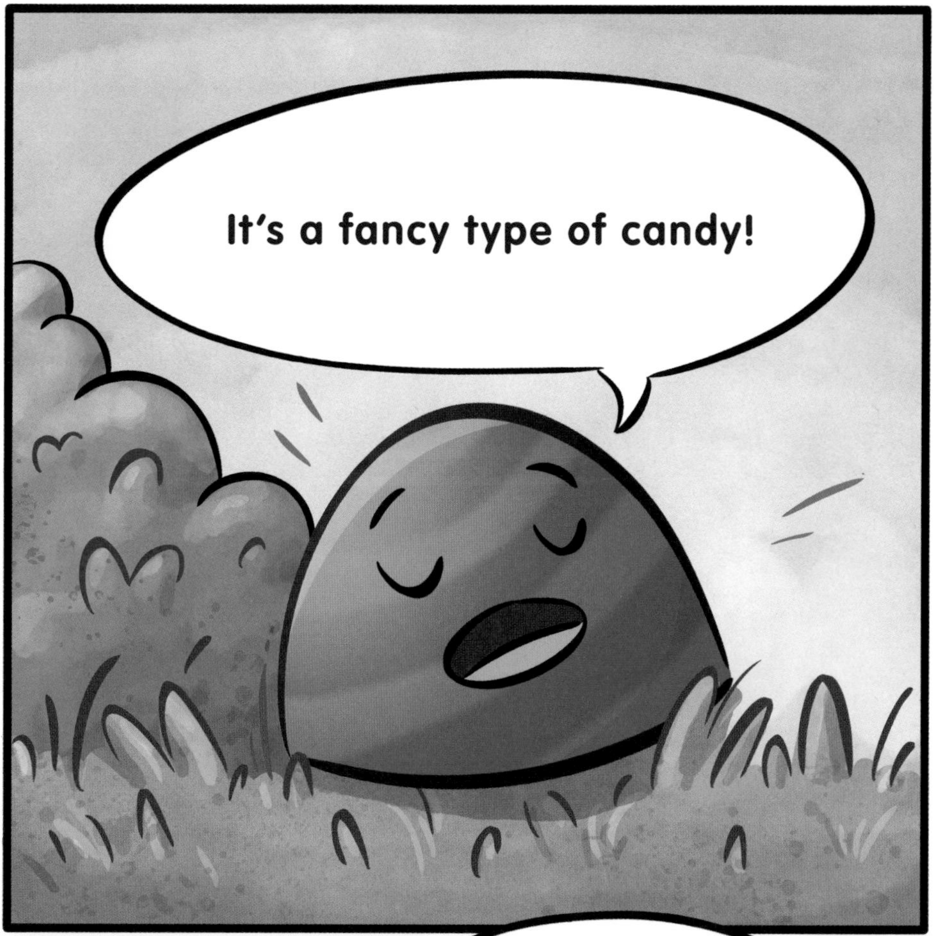
It's a fancy type of candy!

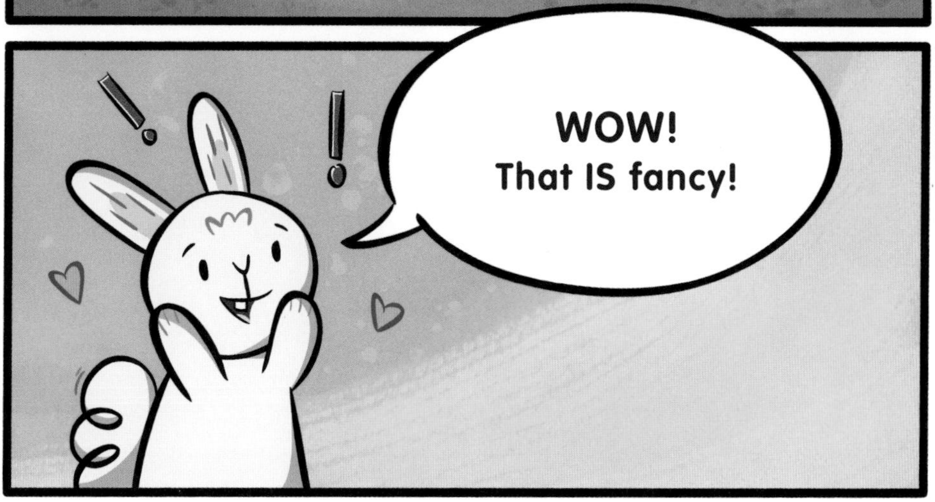
WOW!
That IS fancy!

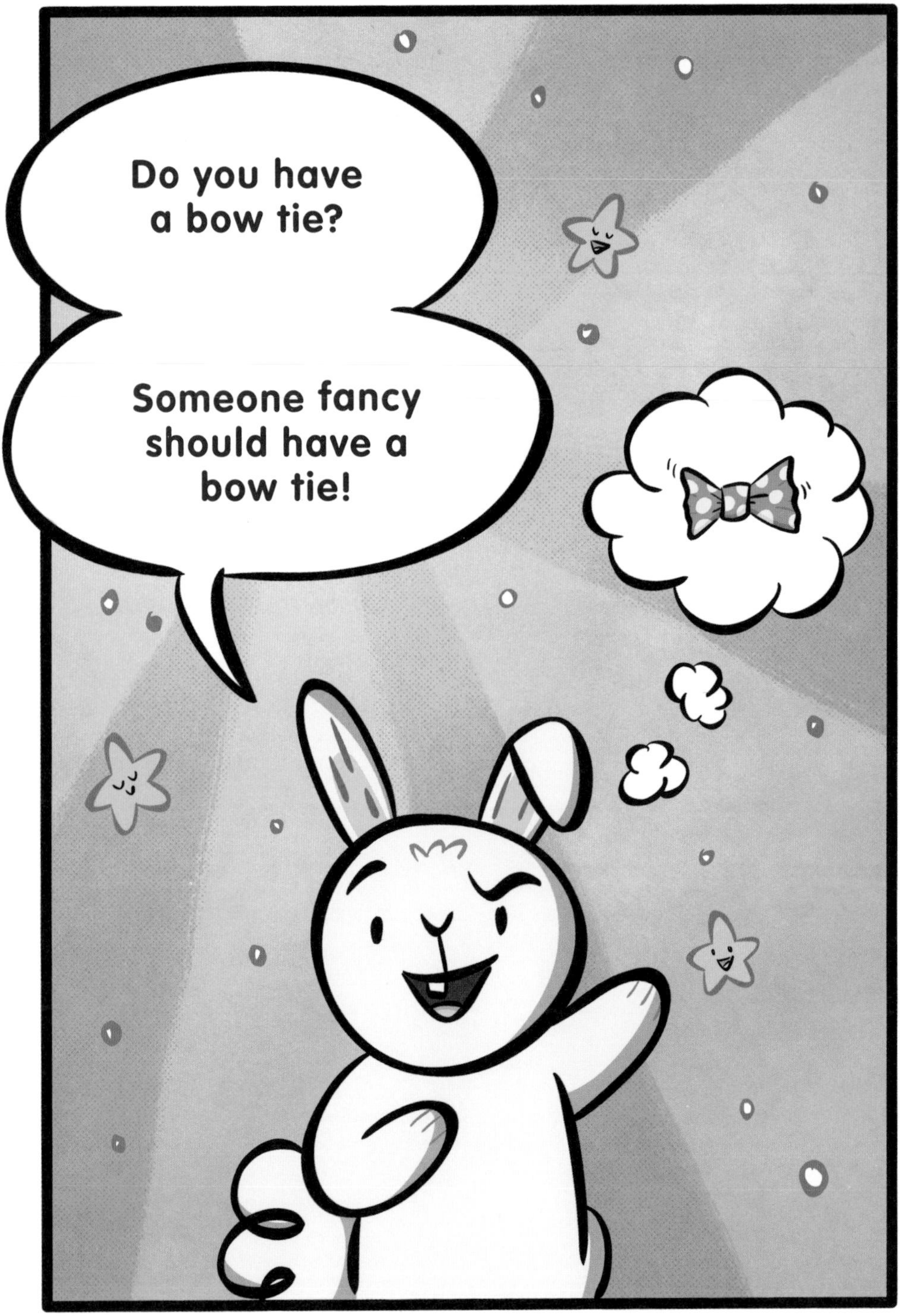
Do you have a bow tie?
Someone fancy should have a bow tie!

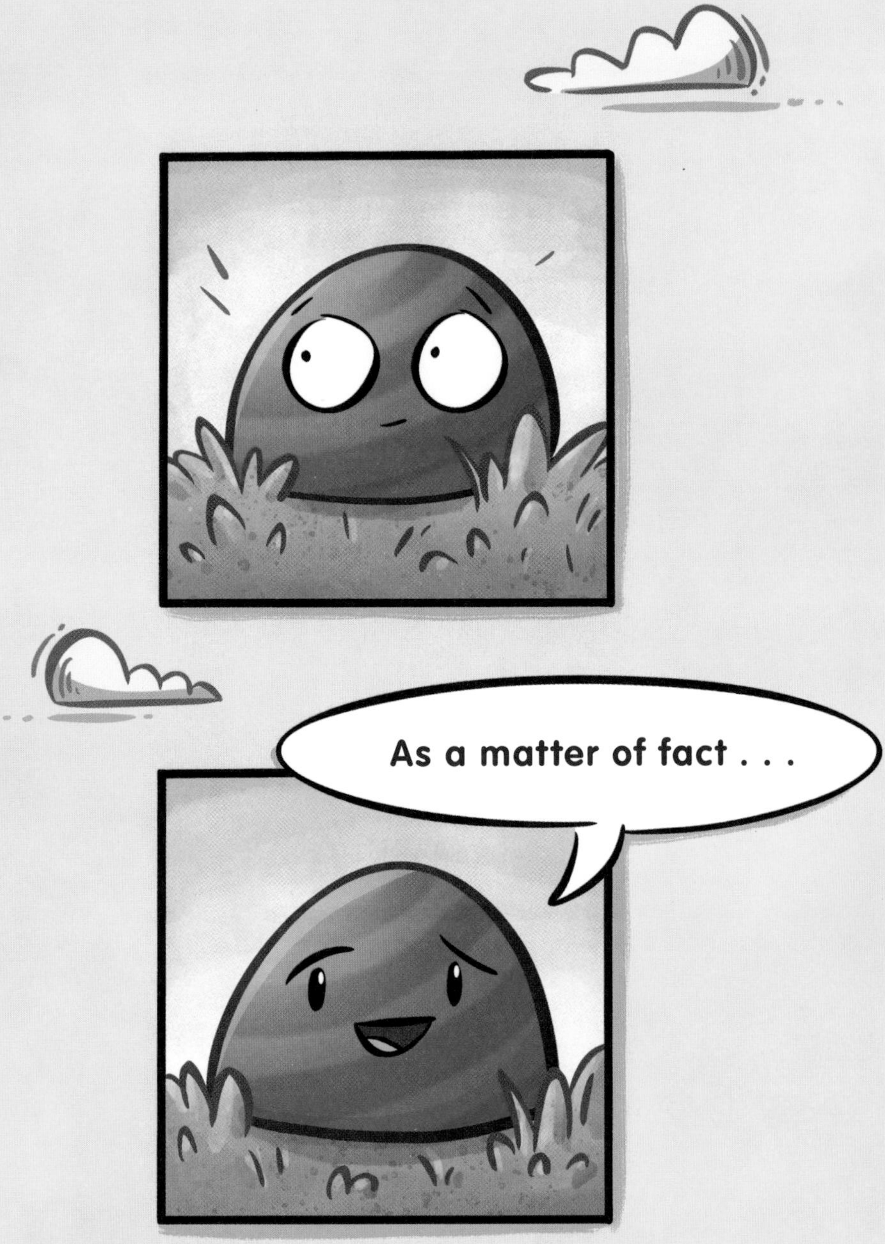
As a matter of fact . . .

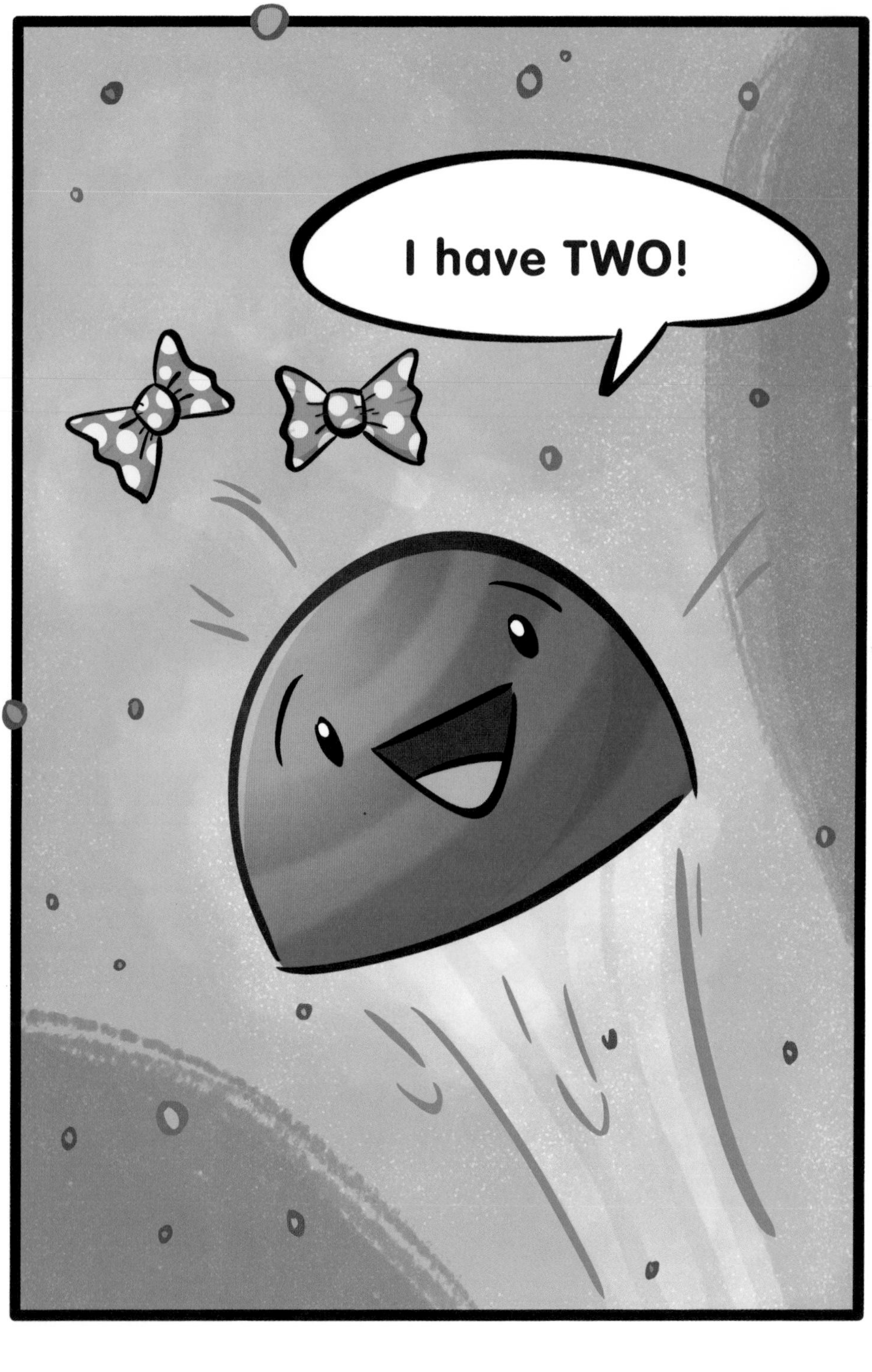
I have TWO!

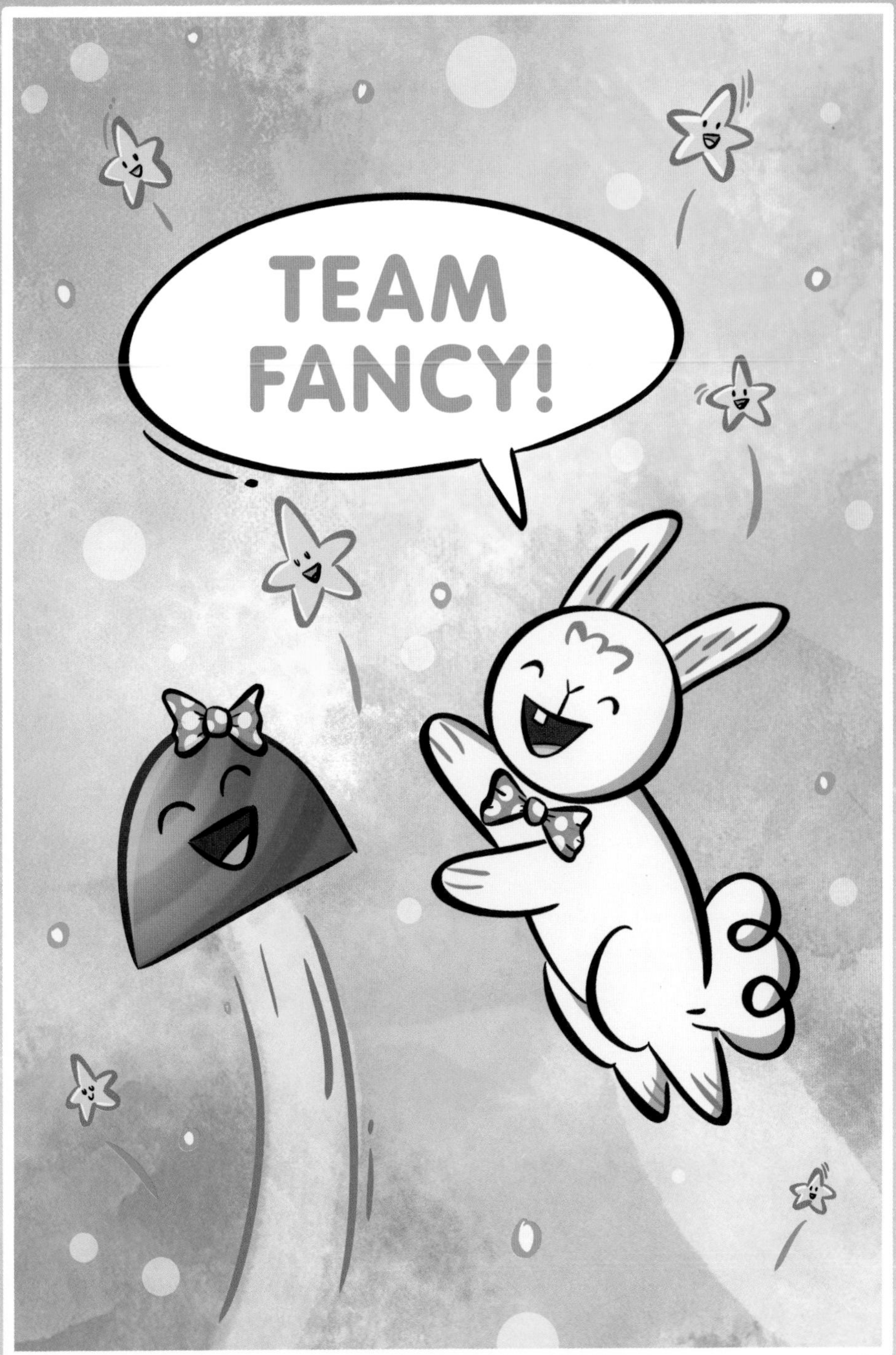
TEAM FANCY!

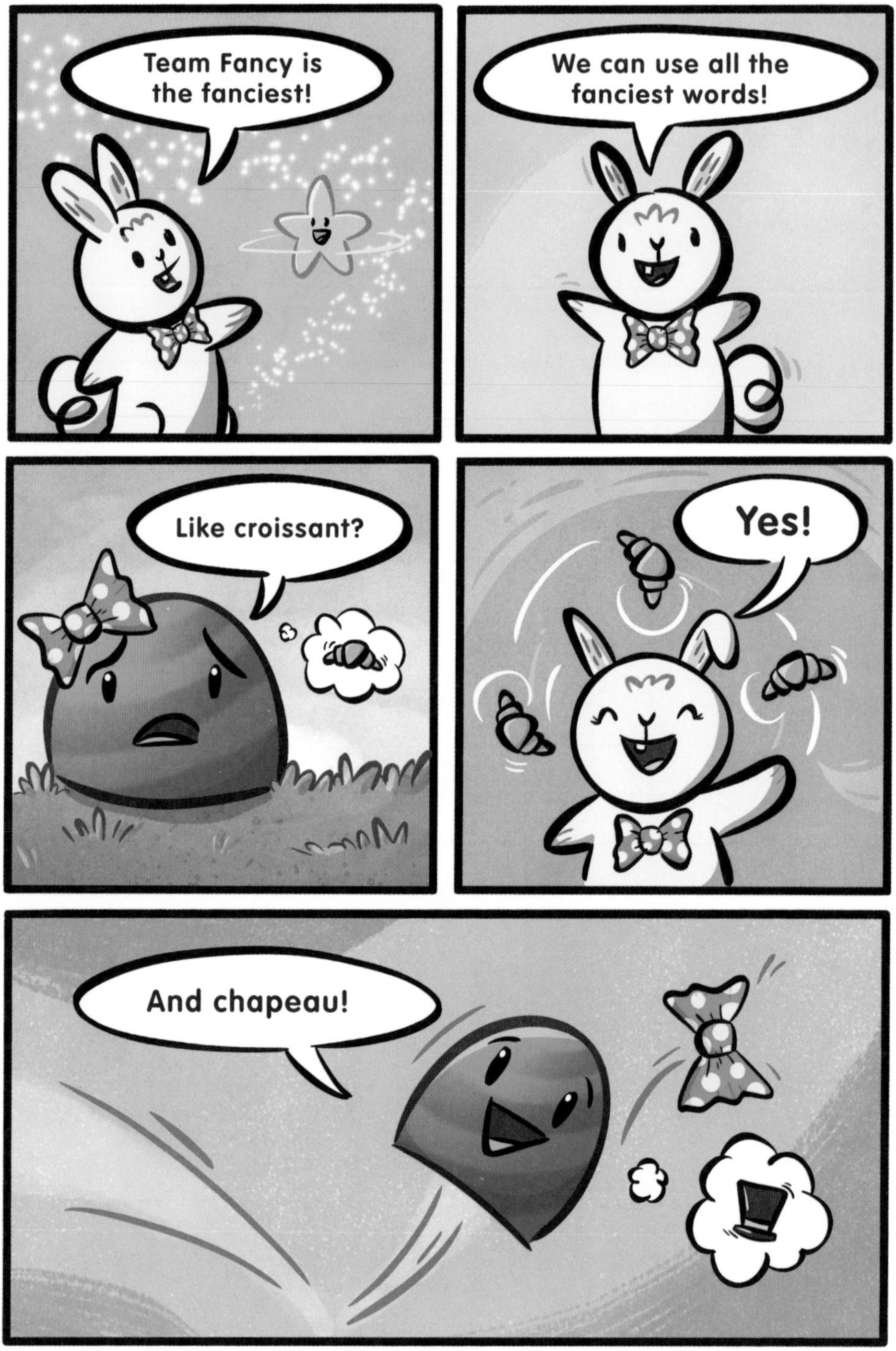
Team Fancy is the fanciest!
We can use all the fanciest words!
Like croissant?
Yes!
And chapeau!

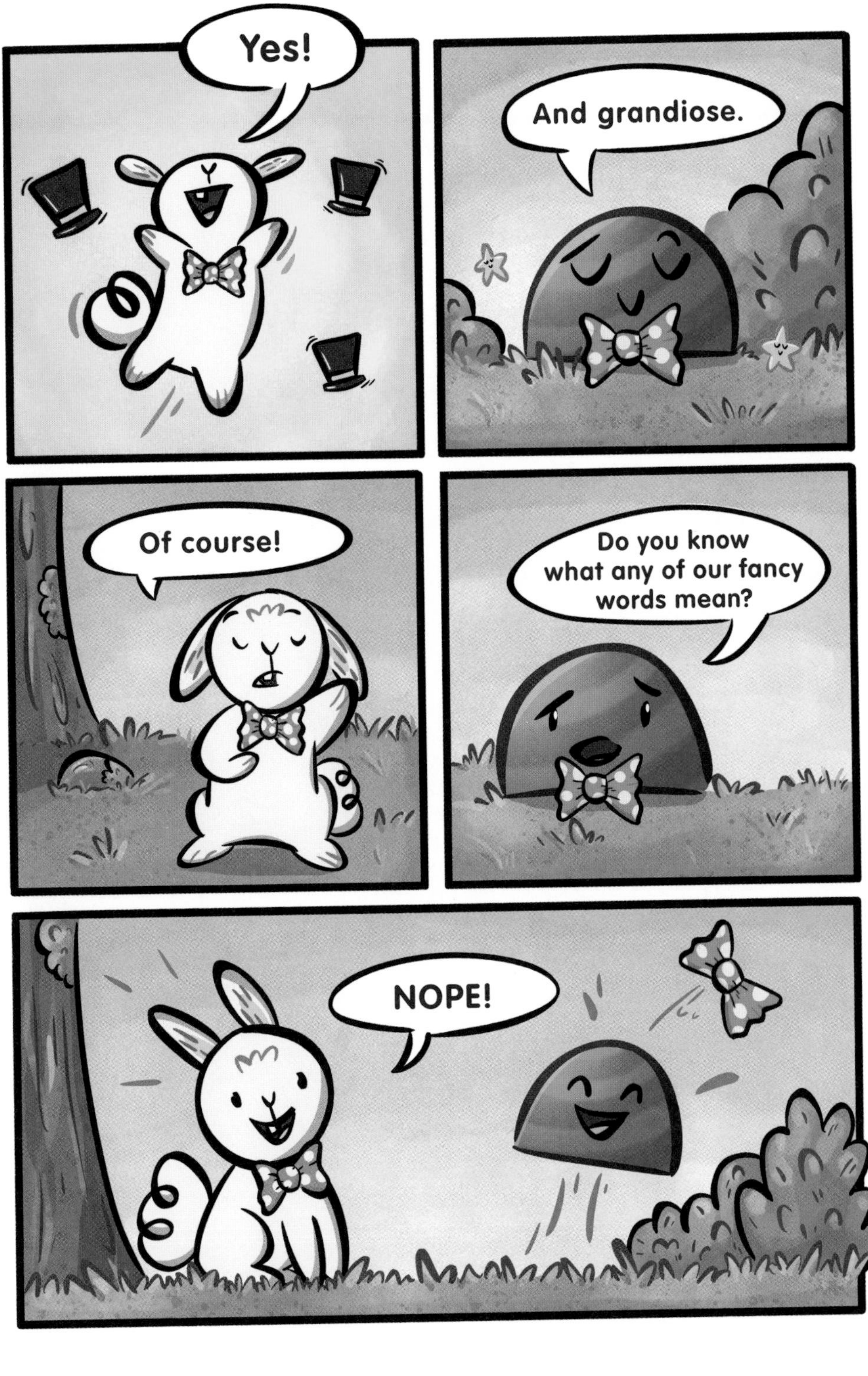
Yes!
And grandiose.
Of course!
Do you know what any of our fancy words mean?
NOPE!

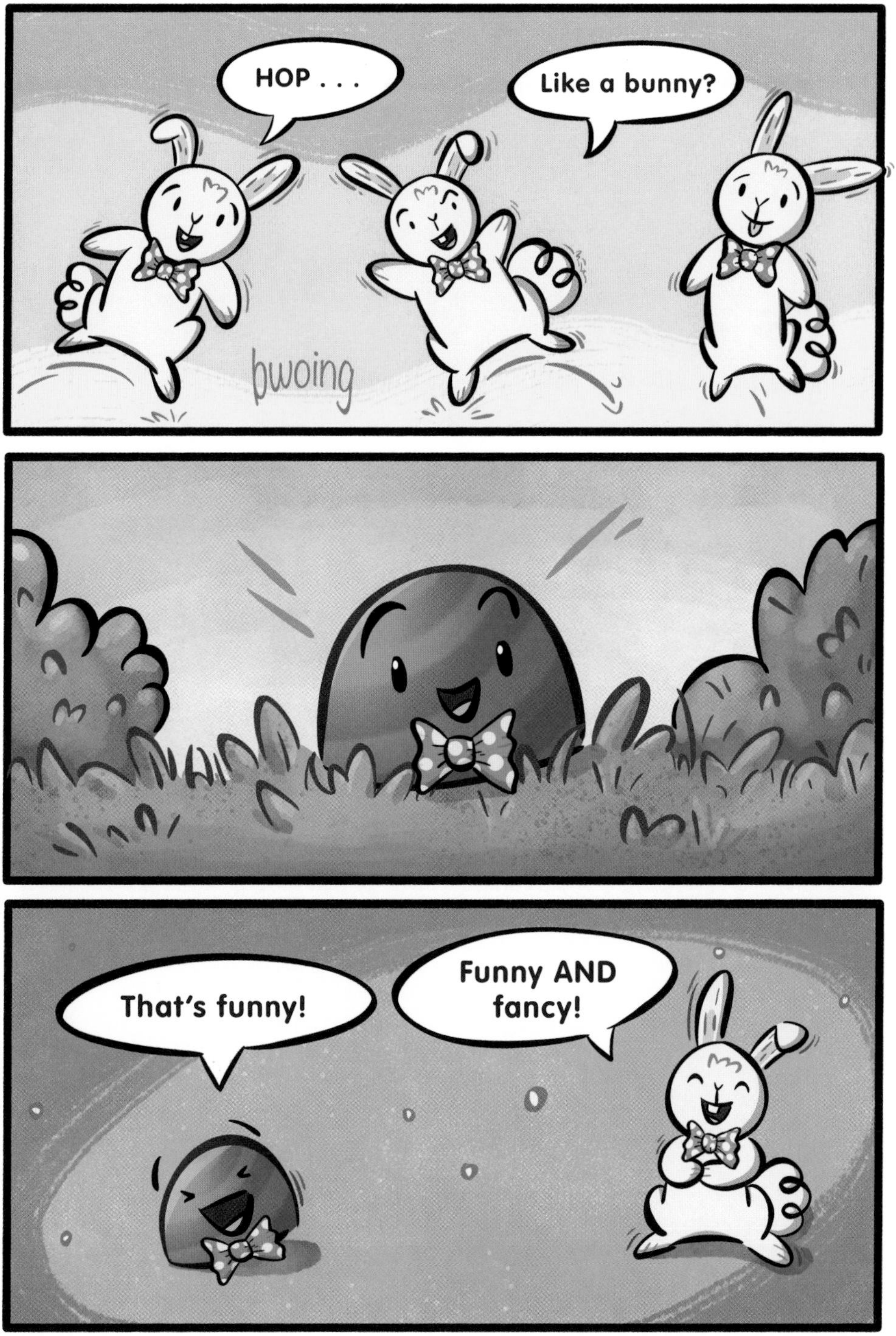
HOP . . .
Like a bunny?
bwoing
That's funny!
Funny AND fancy!

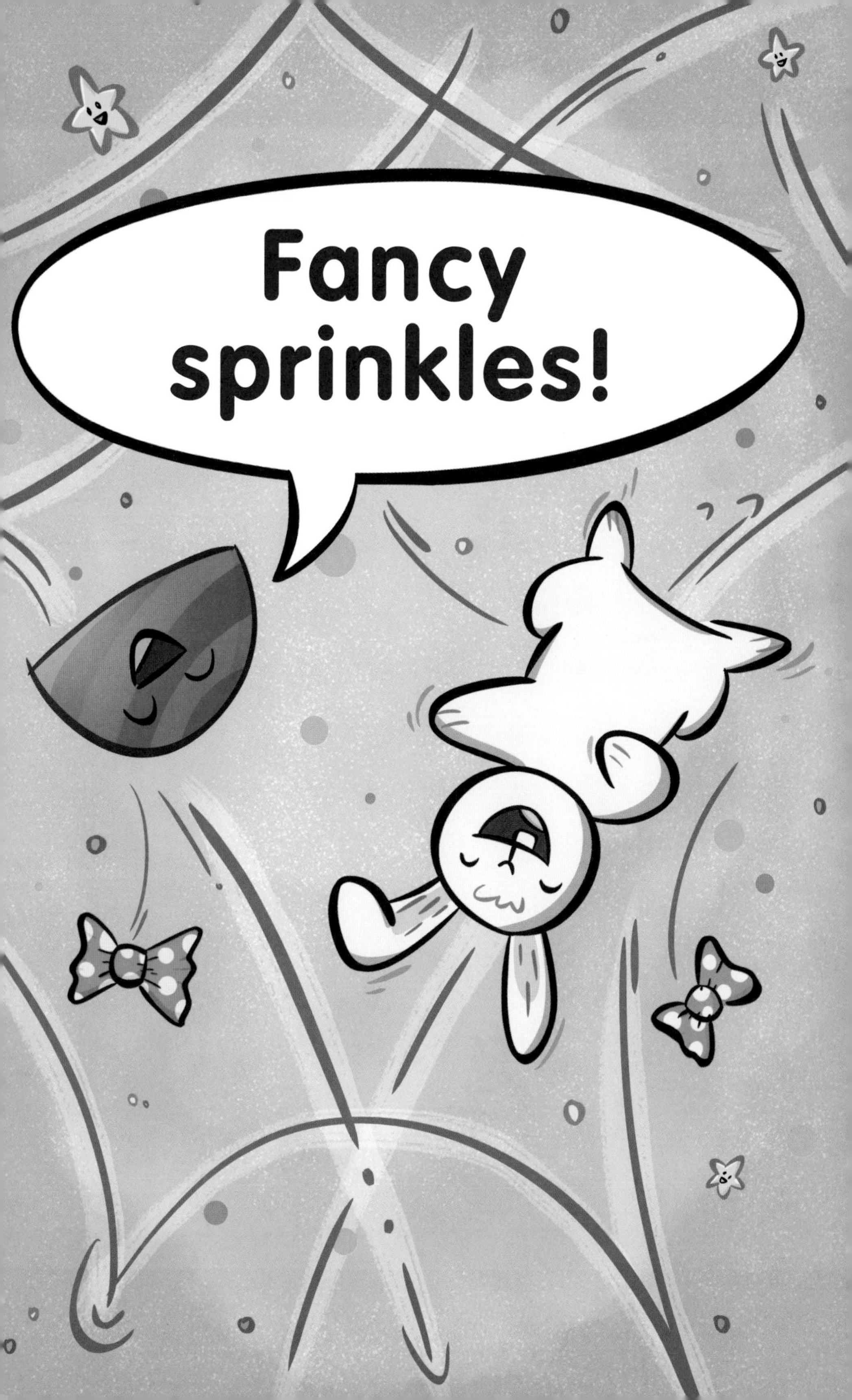
Fancy sprinkles!

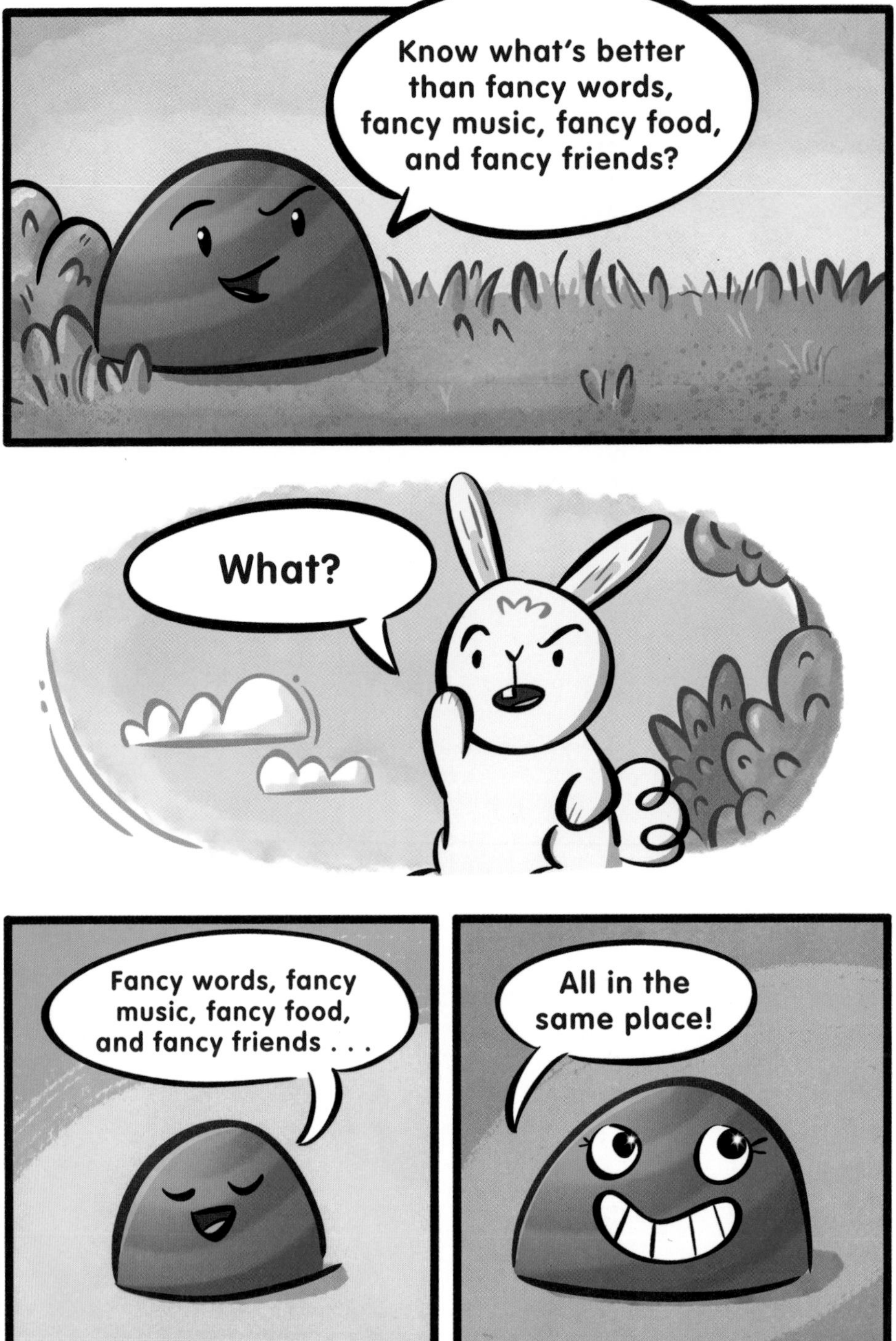
Know what's better than fancy words, fancy music, fancy food, and fancy friends?
What?
Fancy words, fancy music, fancy food, and fancy friends . . .
All in the same place!

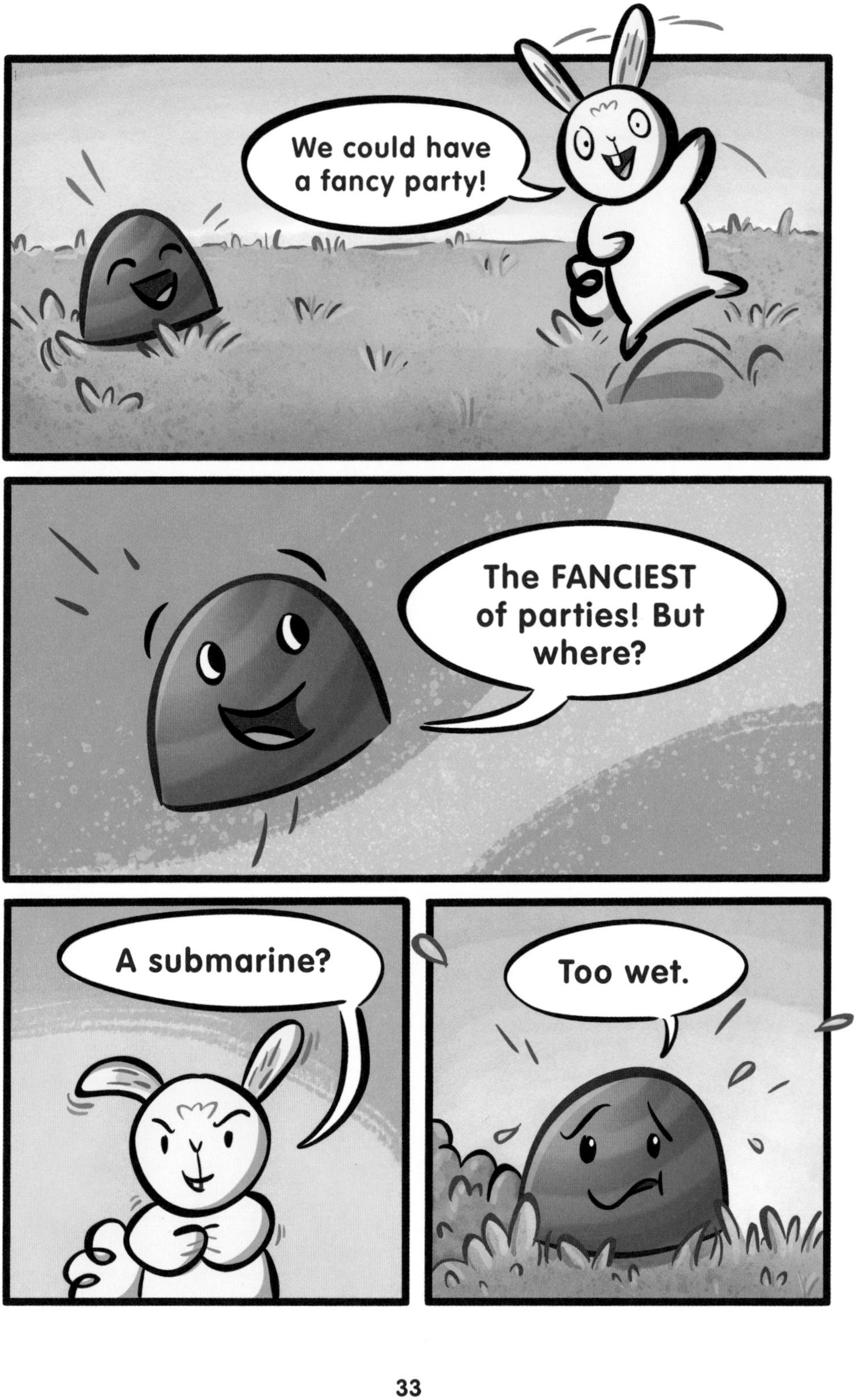
We could have a fancy party!
The FANCIEST of parties! But where?
A submarine?
Too wet.

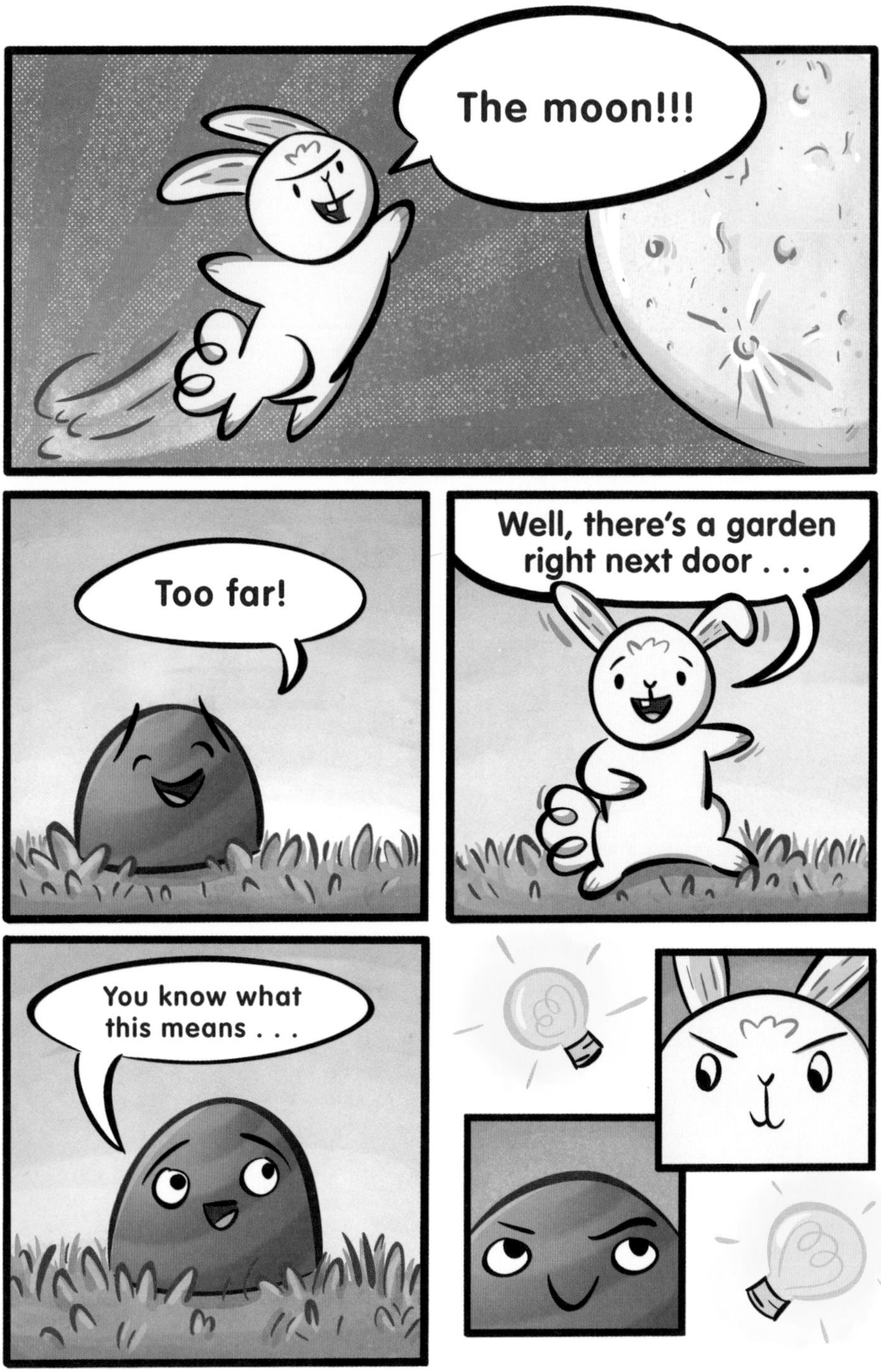
The moon!!!
Too far!
Well, there's a garden right next door . . .
You know what this means . . .

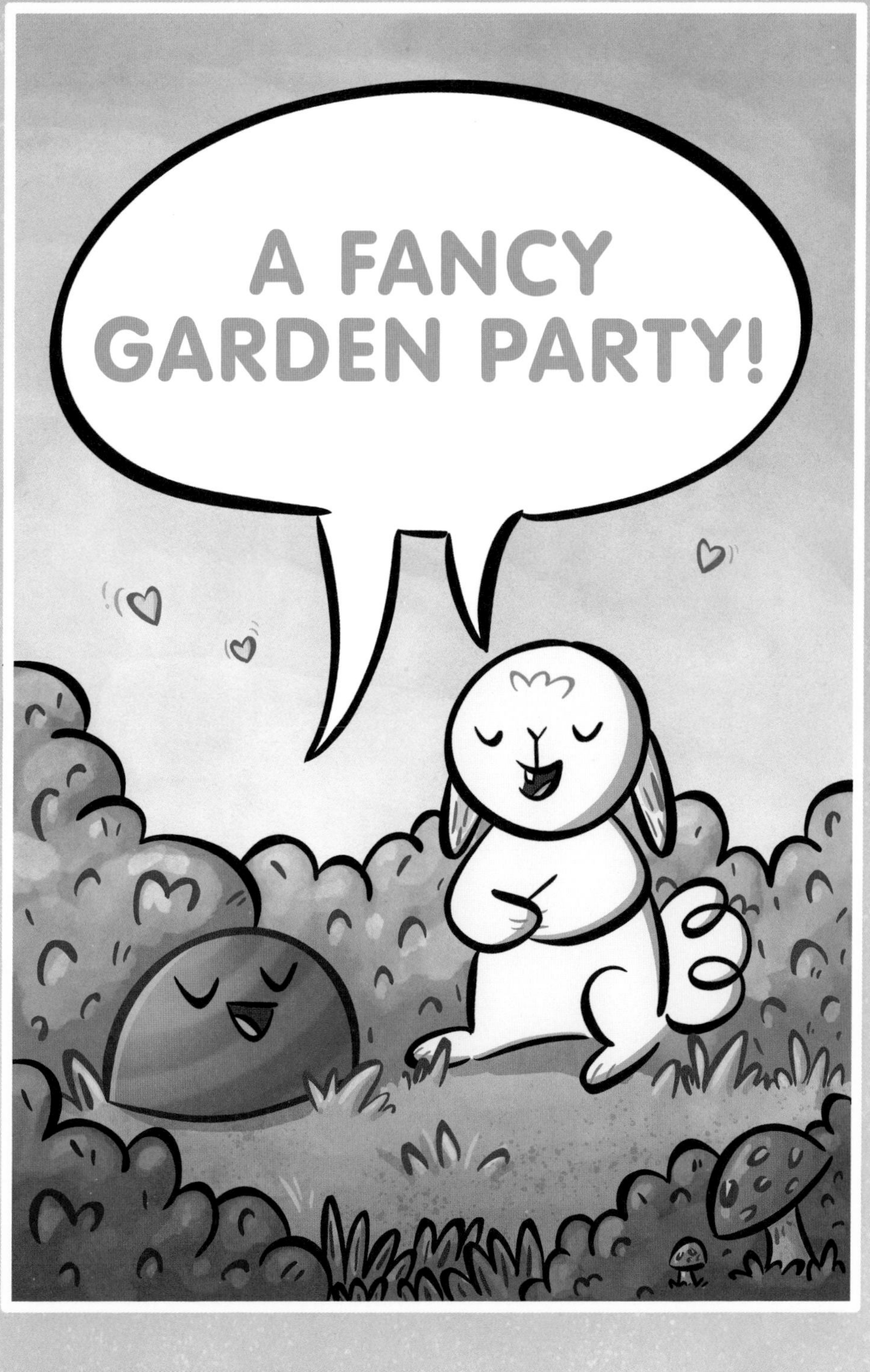
A FANCY GARDEN PARTY!

36

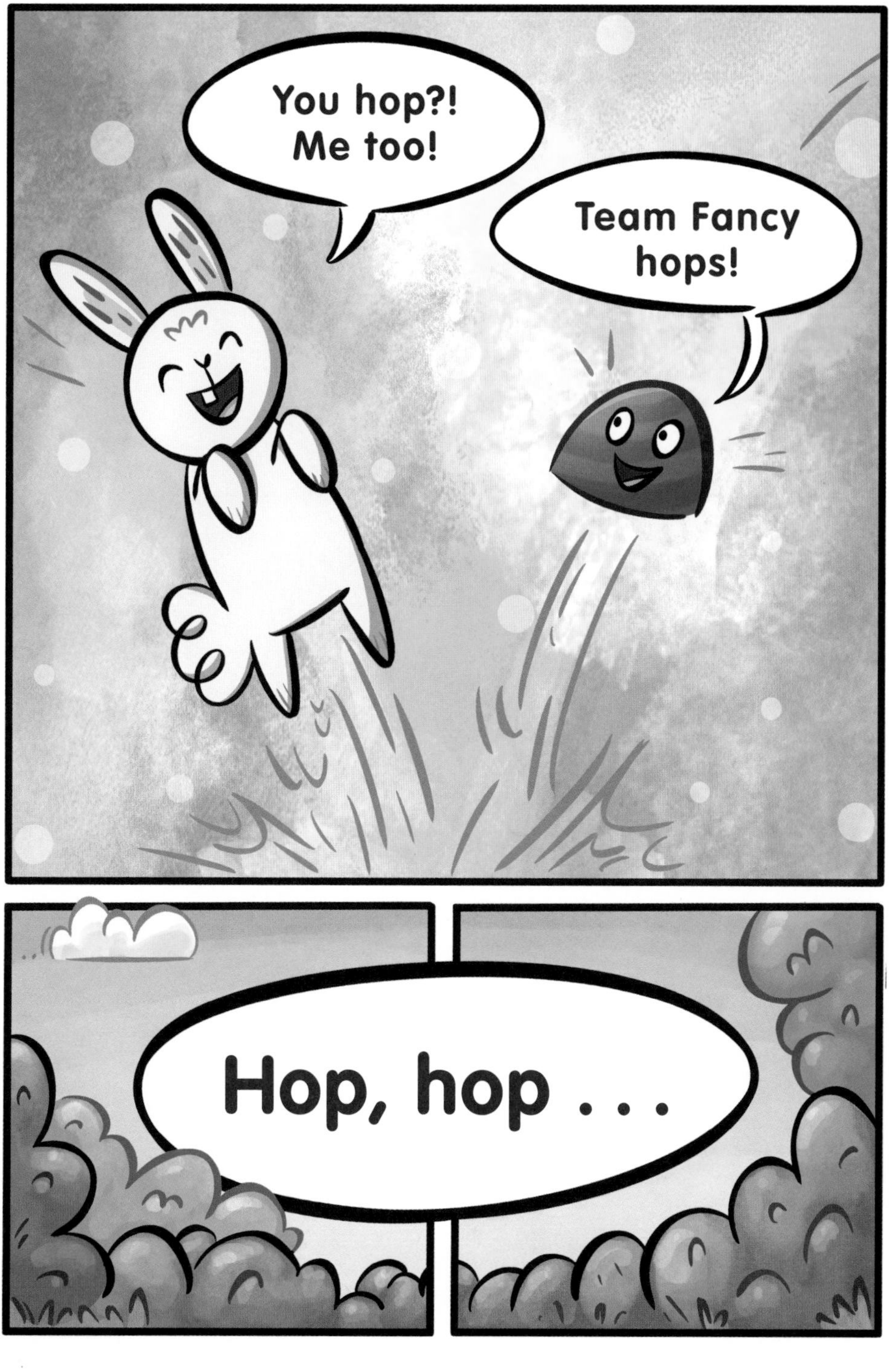
You hop?! Me too!
Team Fancy hops!
Hop, hop . . .

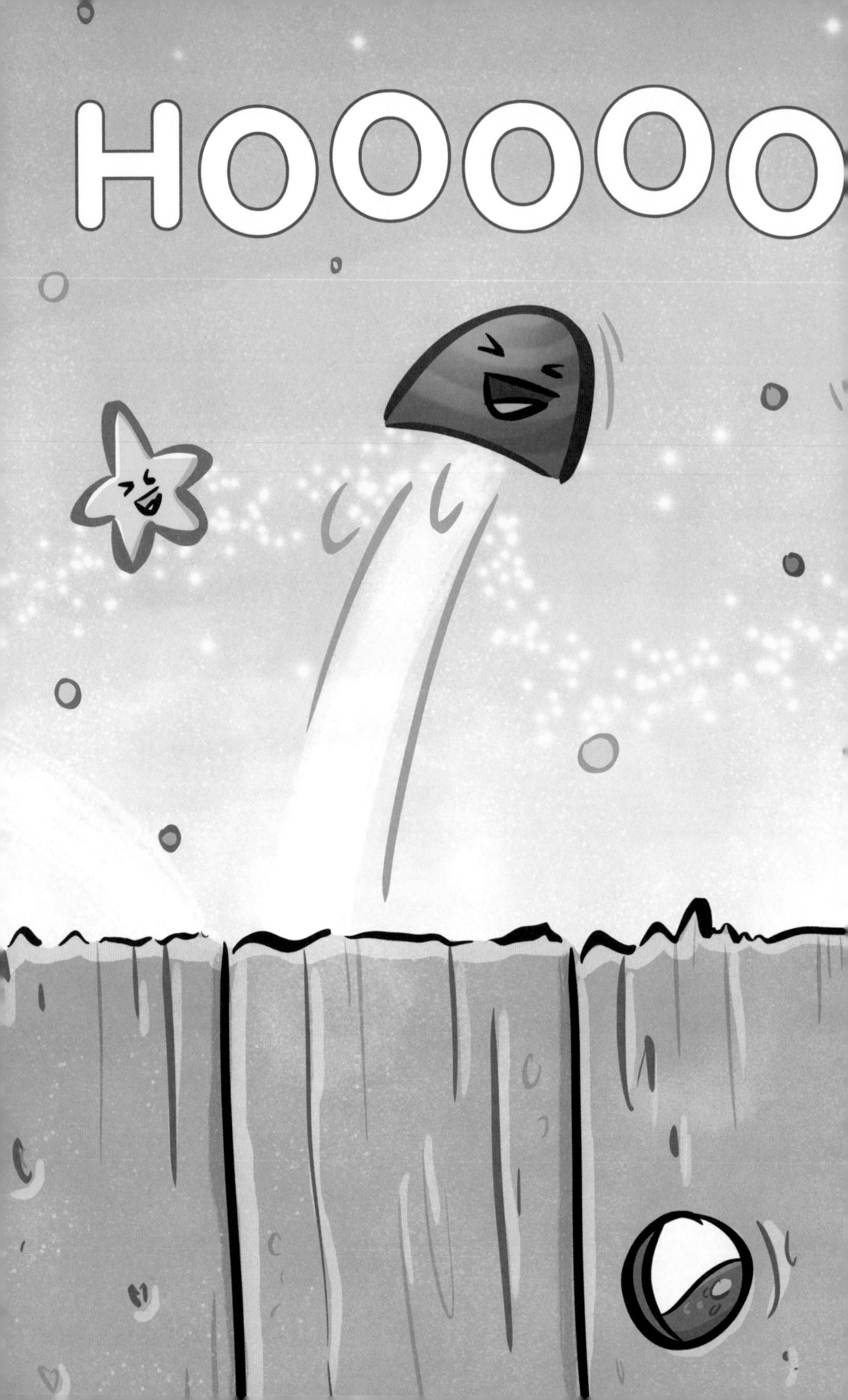
HOOOOO

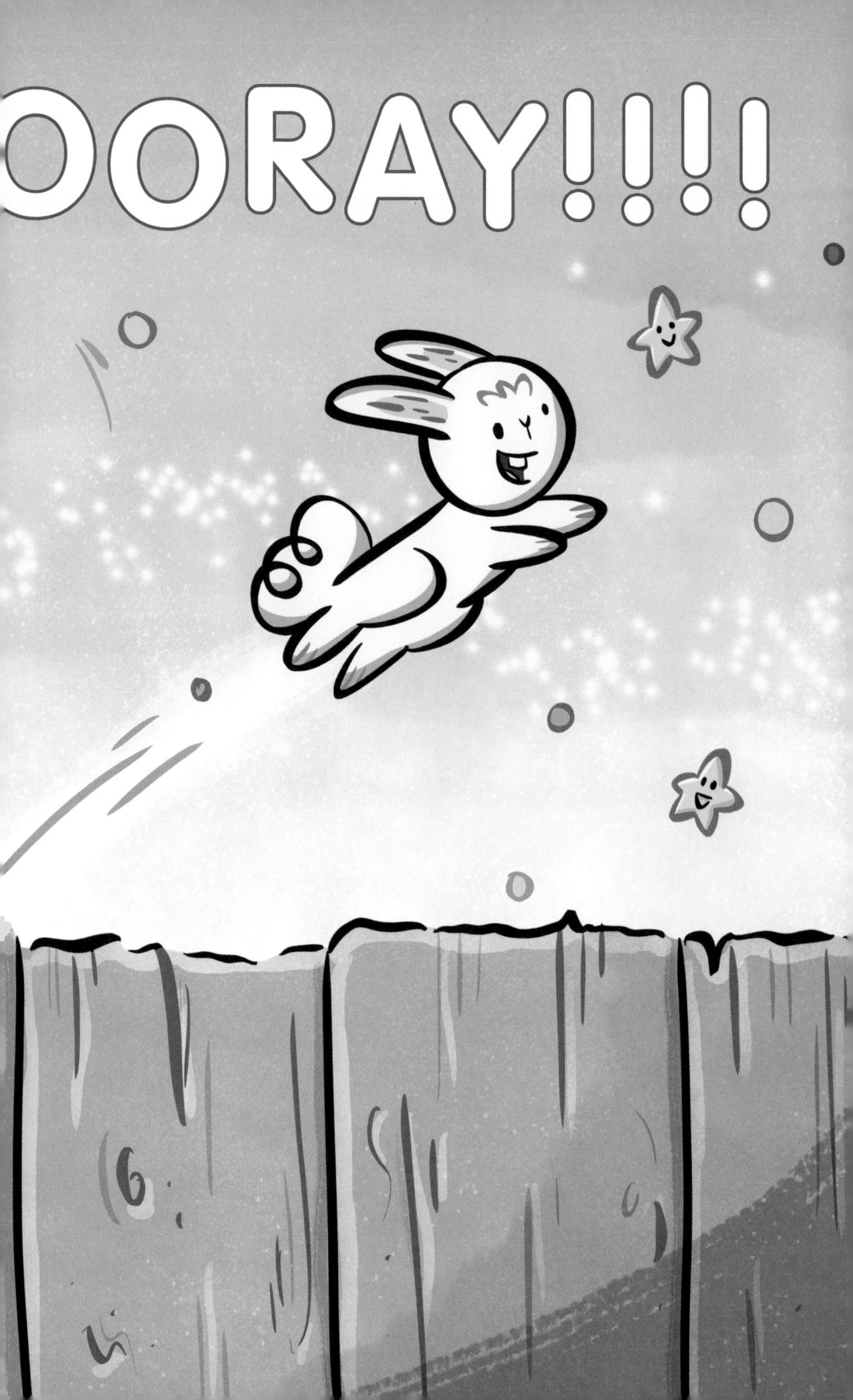
OORAY!!!!

40

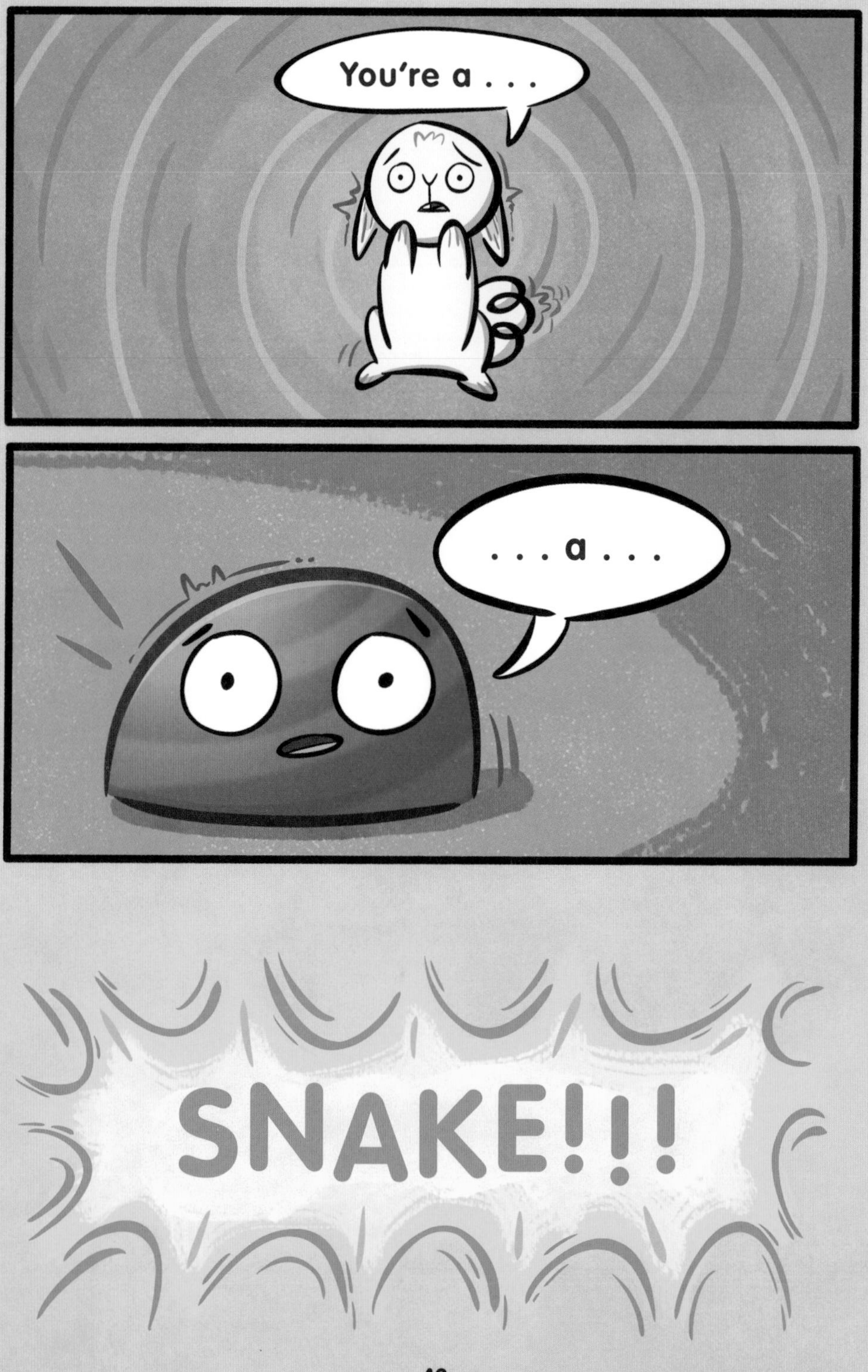
You're a . . .
. . . a . . .
SNAKE!!!

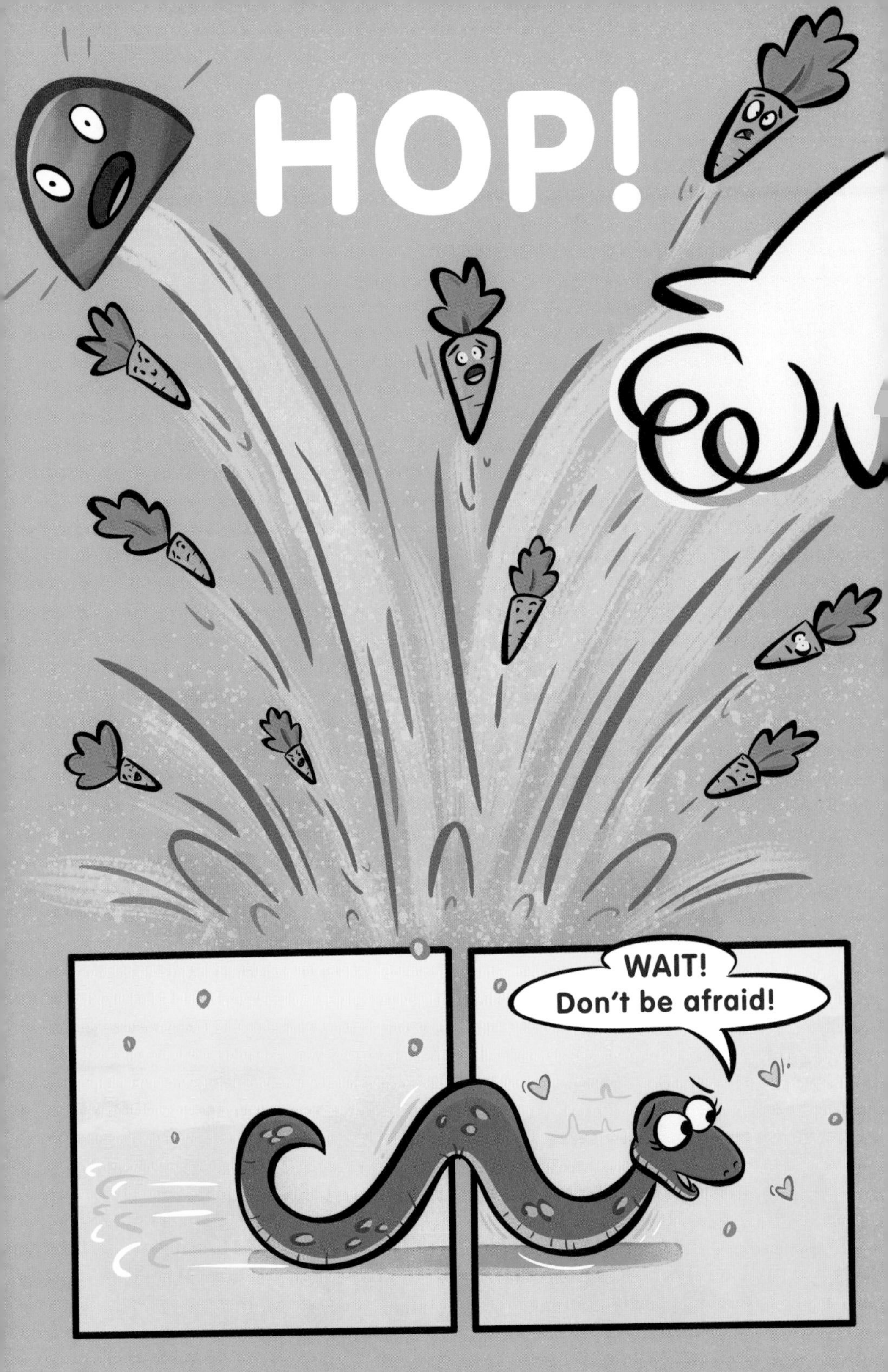
HOP!
WAIT!
Don't be afraid!

44

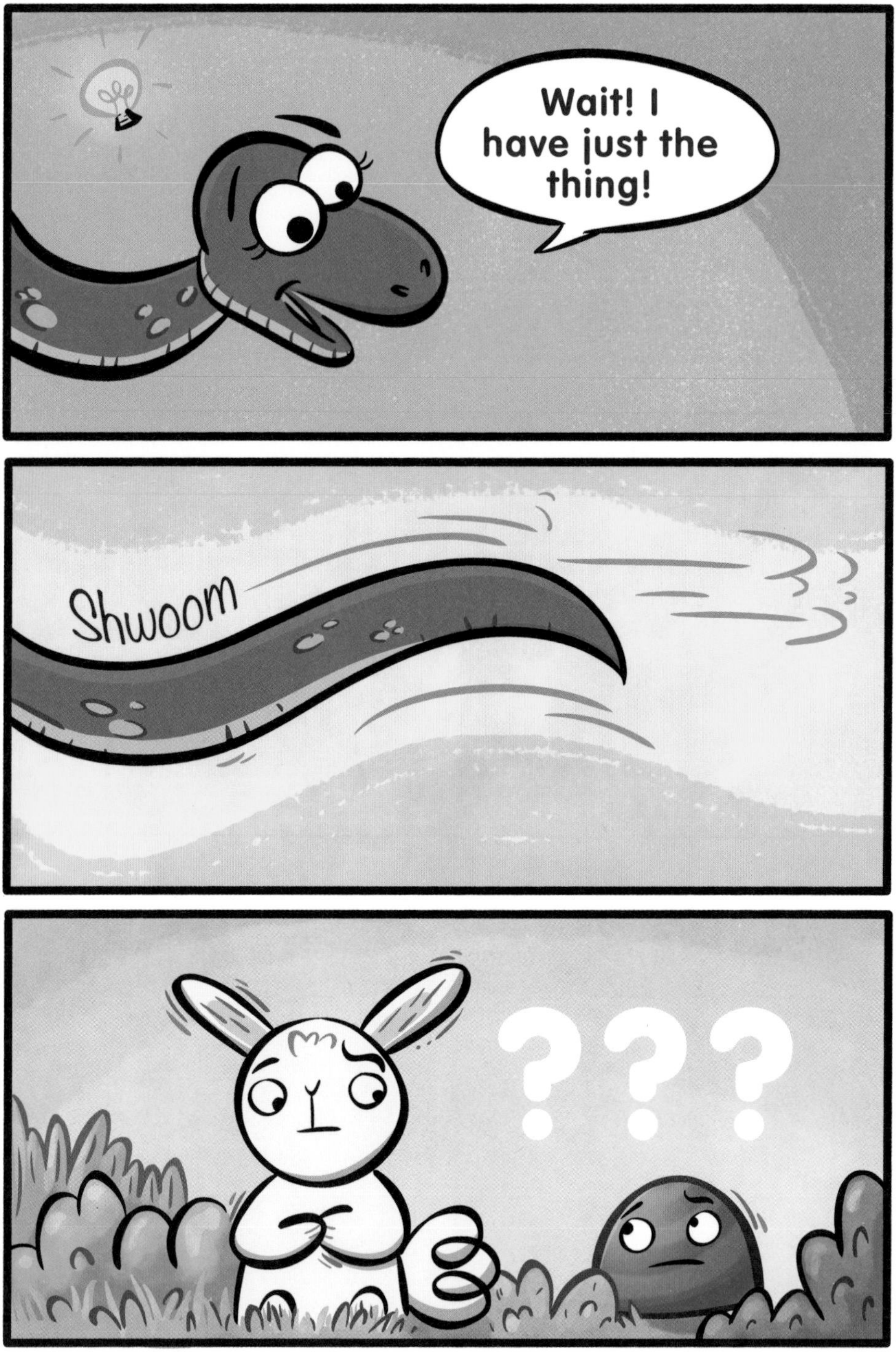
Wait! I have just the thing!
Shwoom
???

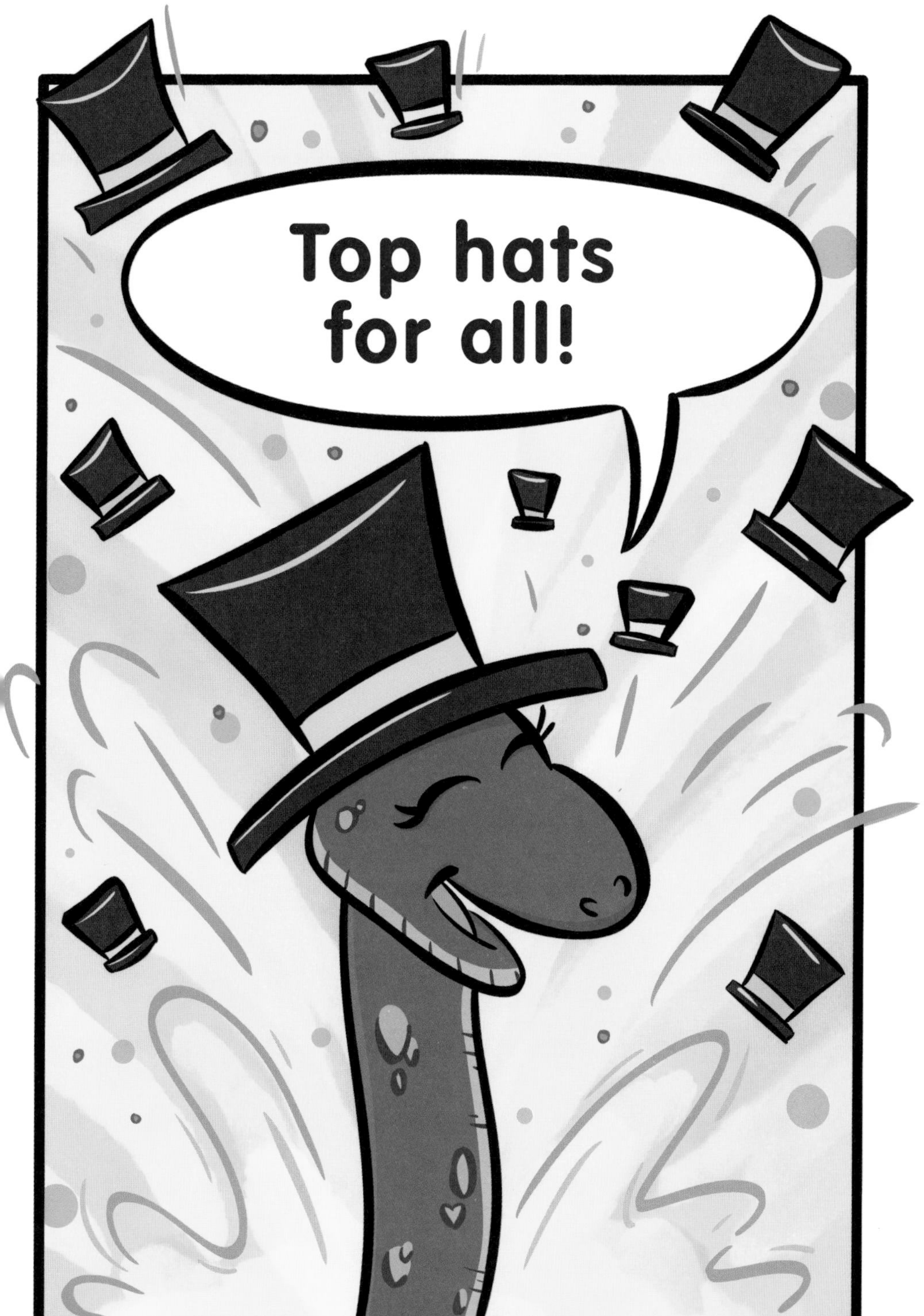
Top hats for all!

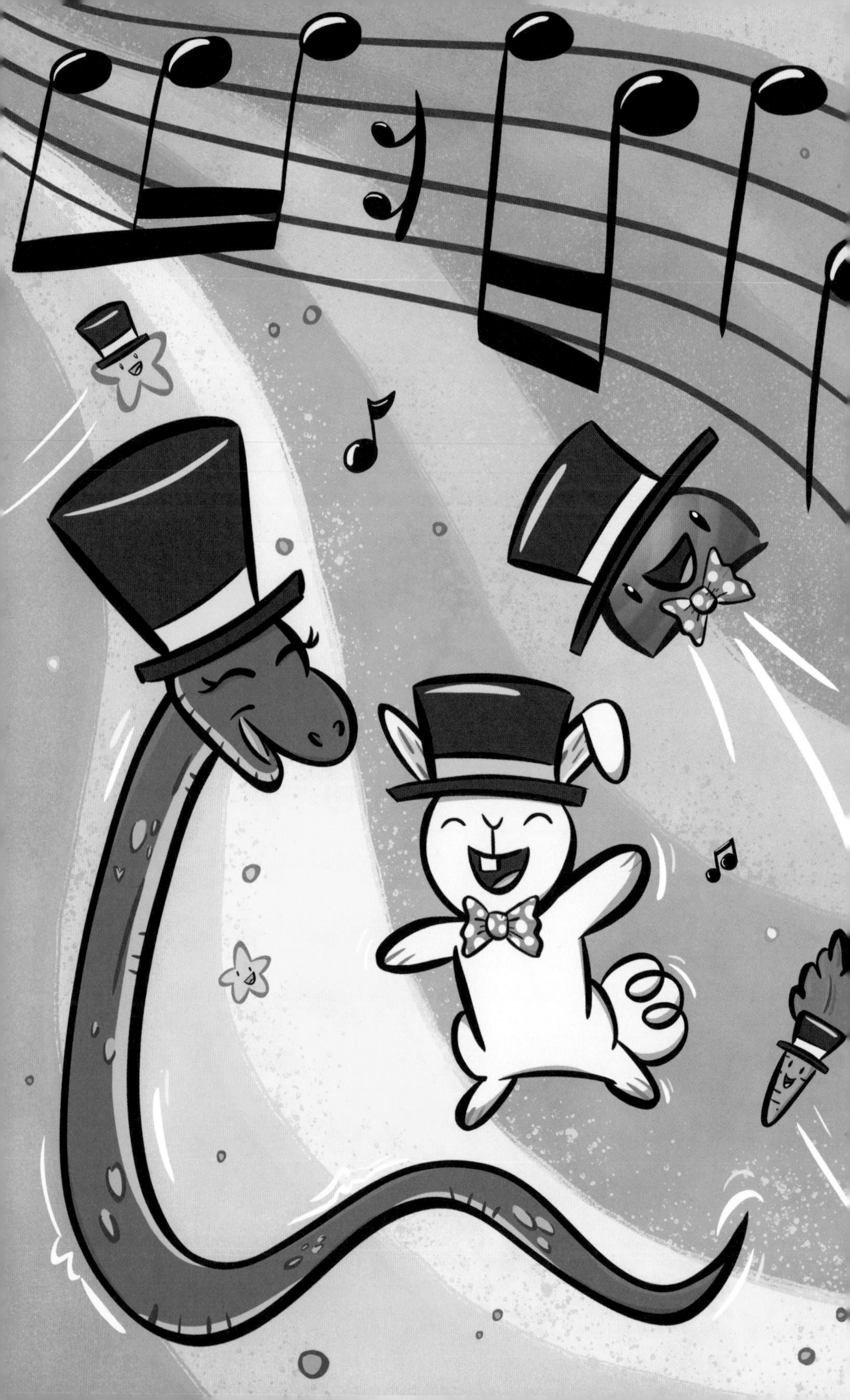

# DONUTS FOR LUNCH!

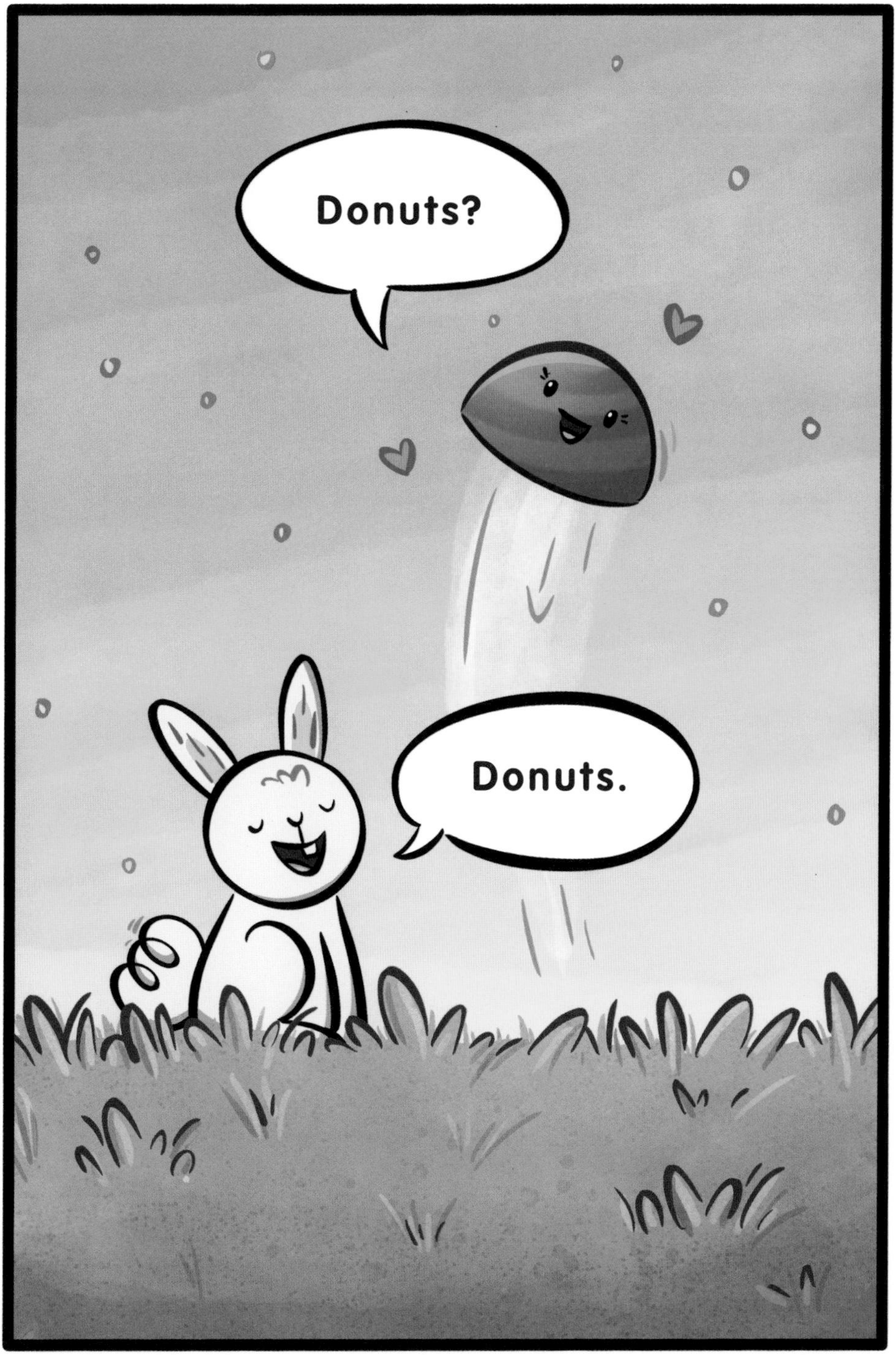
Donuts?
Donuts.

54

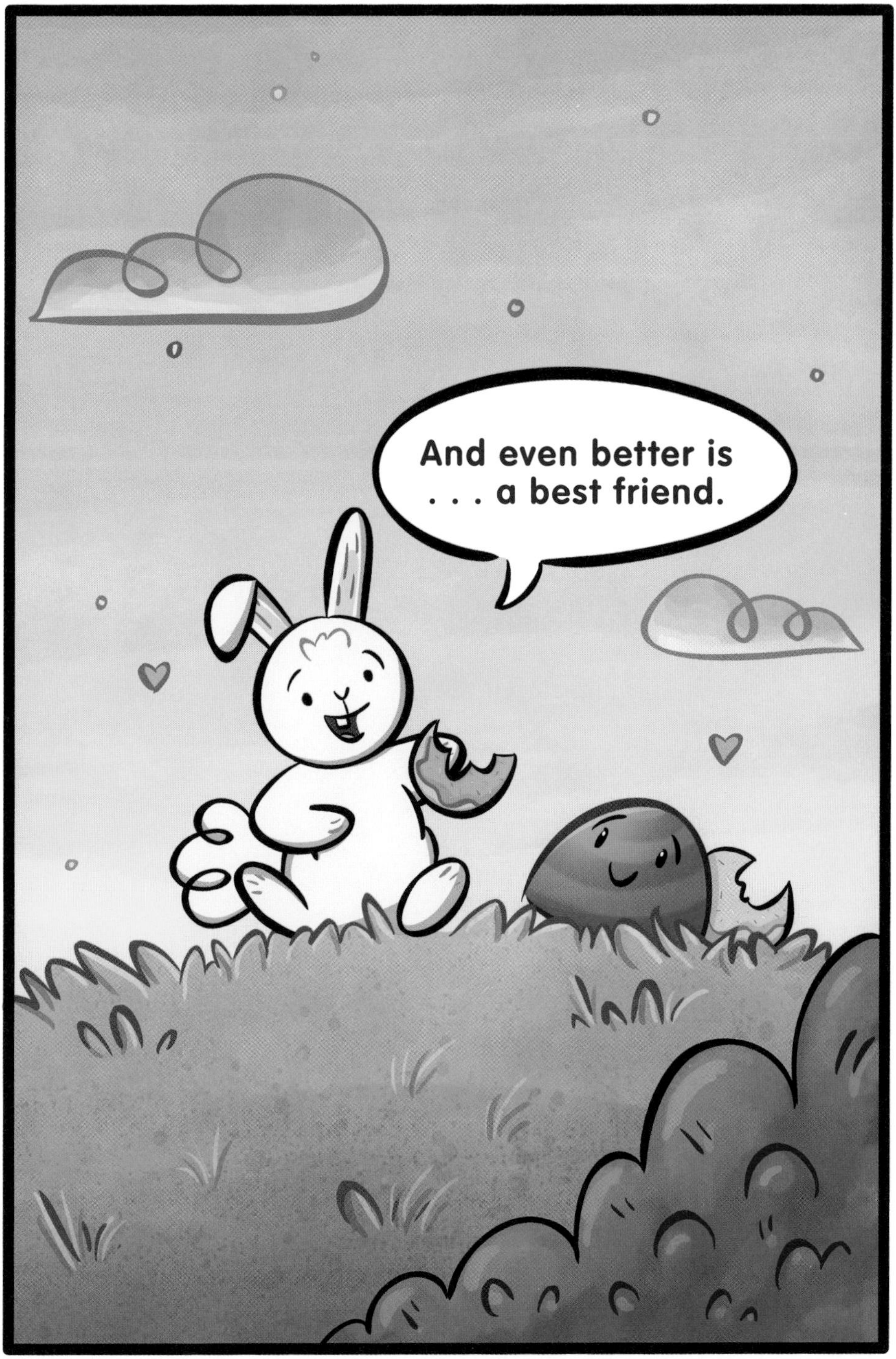
And even better is
. . . a best friend.

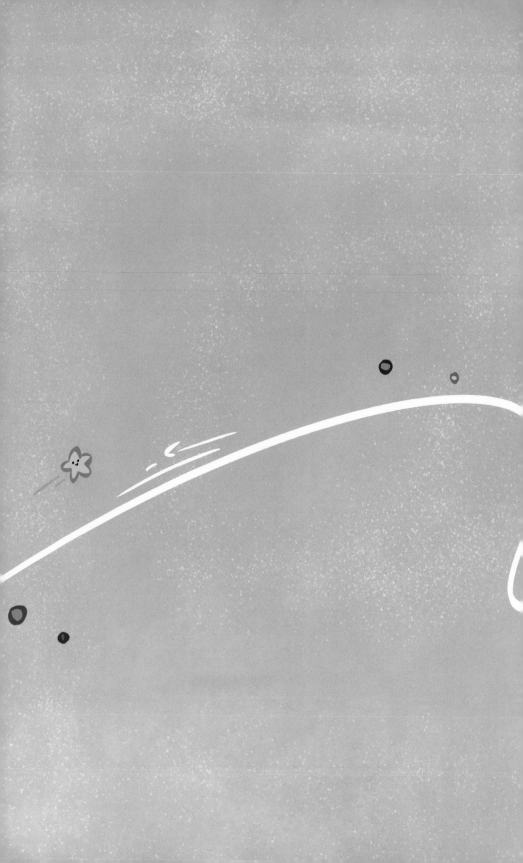

BEST FRIENDS FOREVER AND EVER!

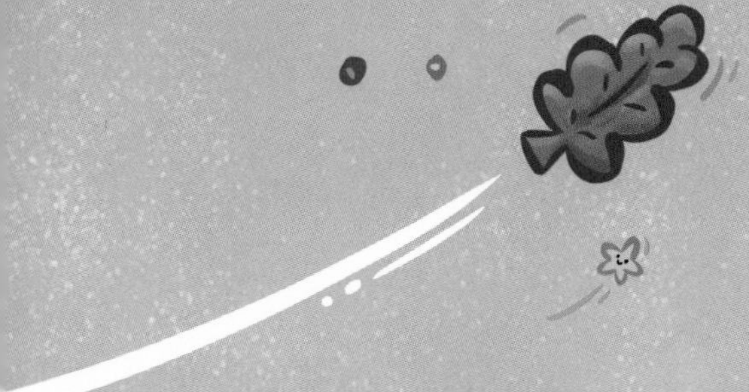

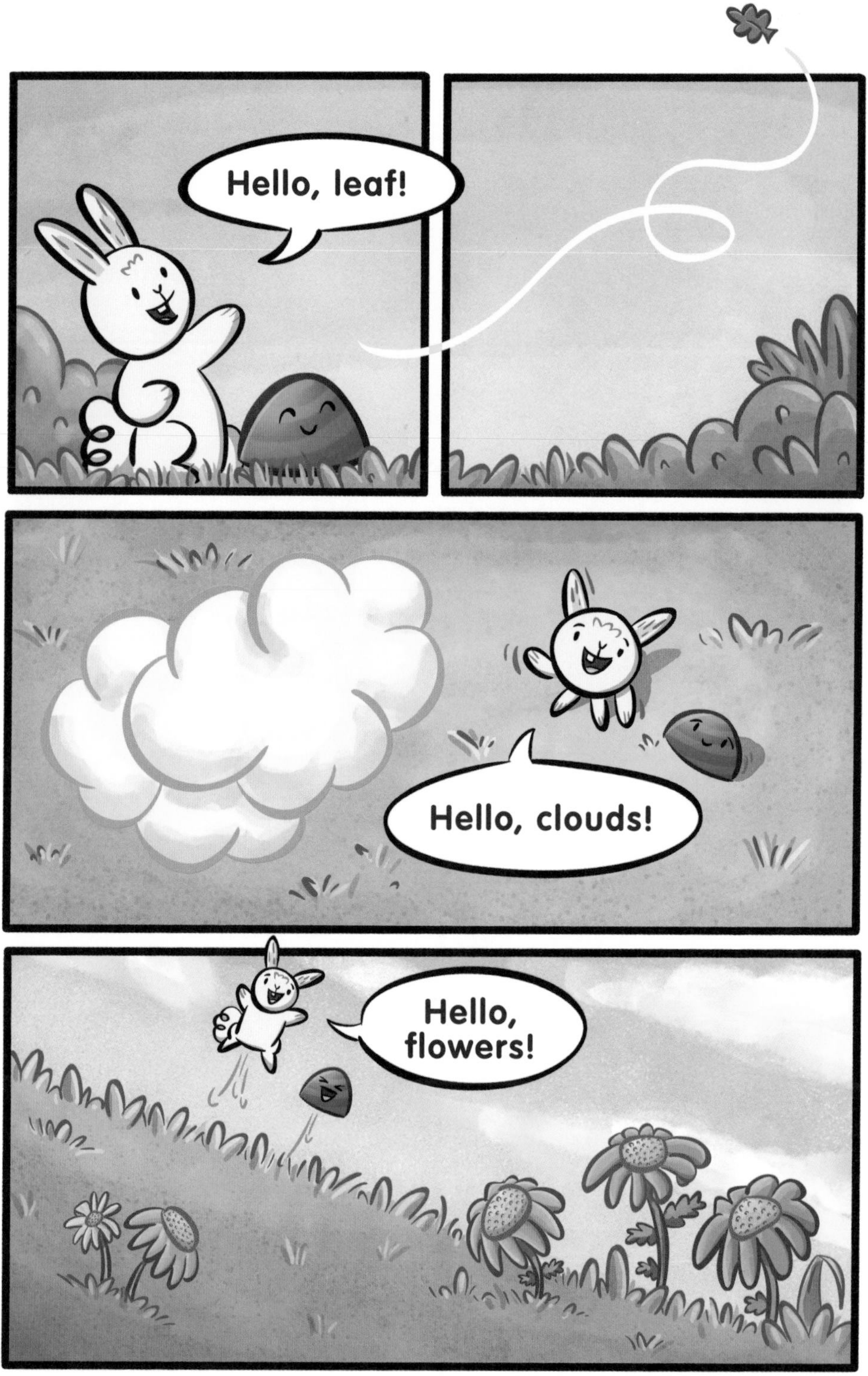
Hello, leaf!
Hello, clouds!
Hello, flowers!

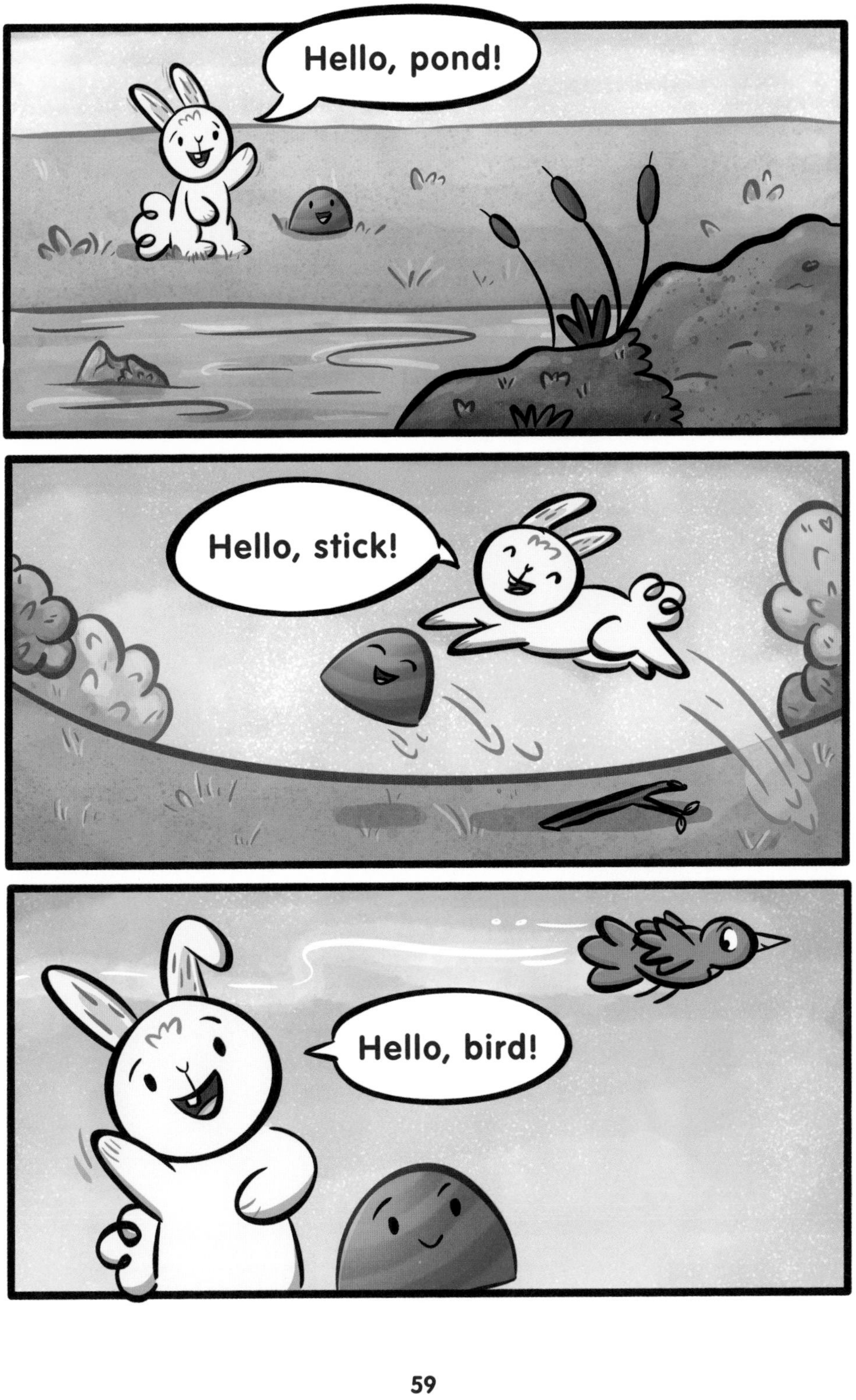
Hello, pond!
Hello, stick!
Hello, bird!

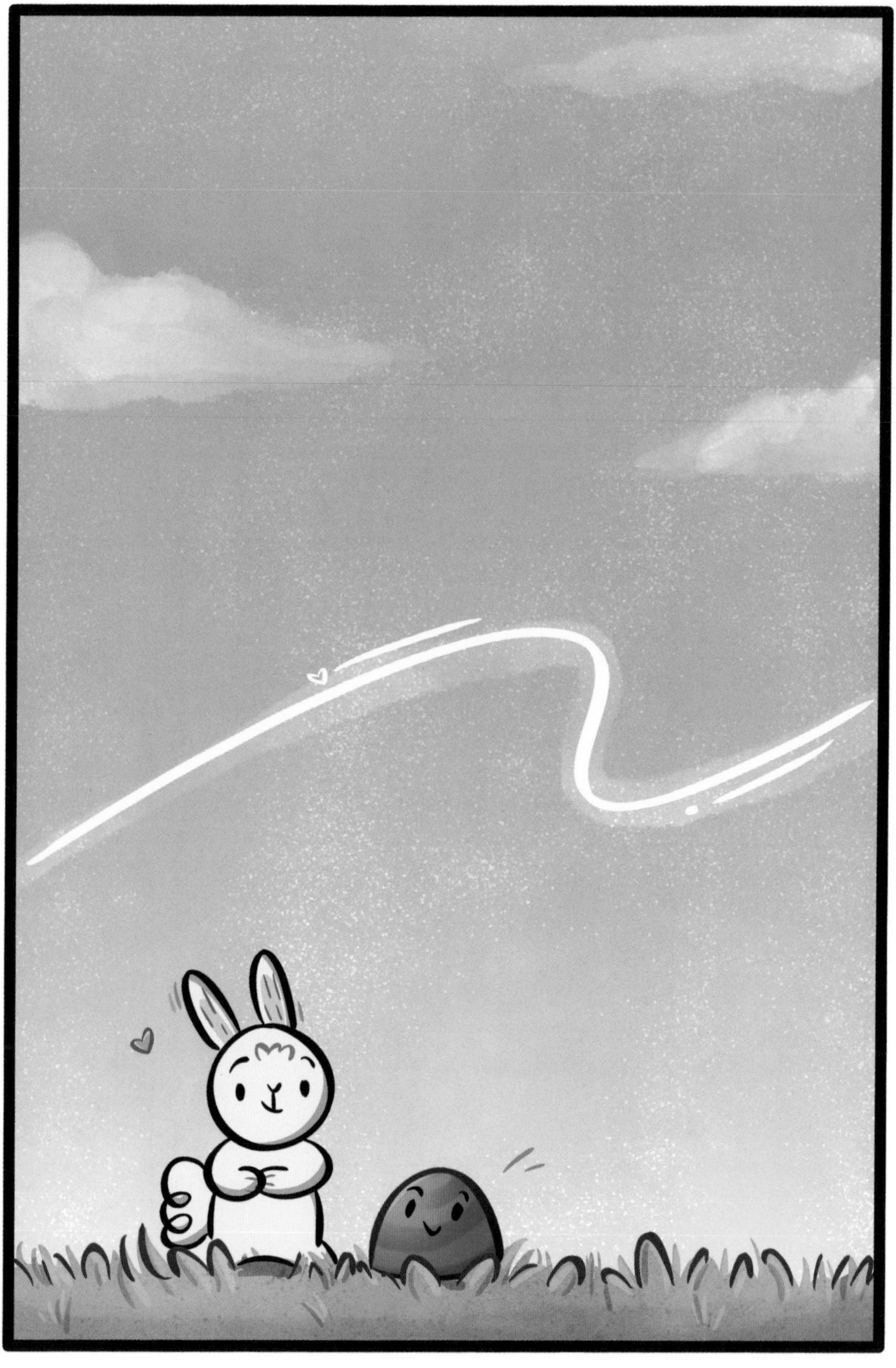

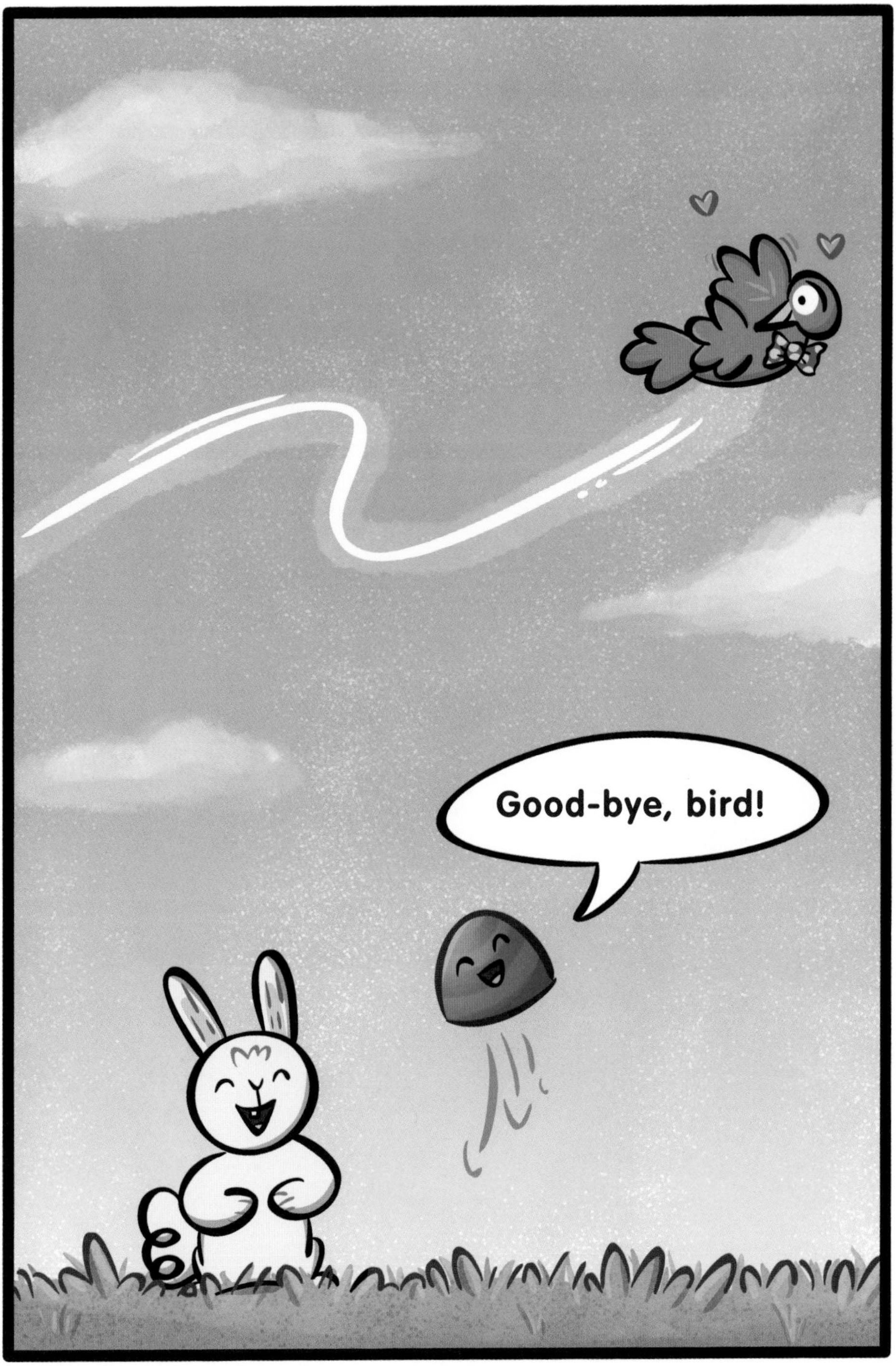
Good-bye, bird!

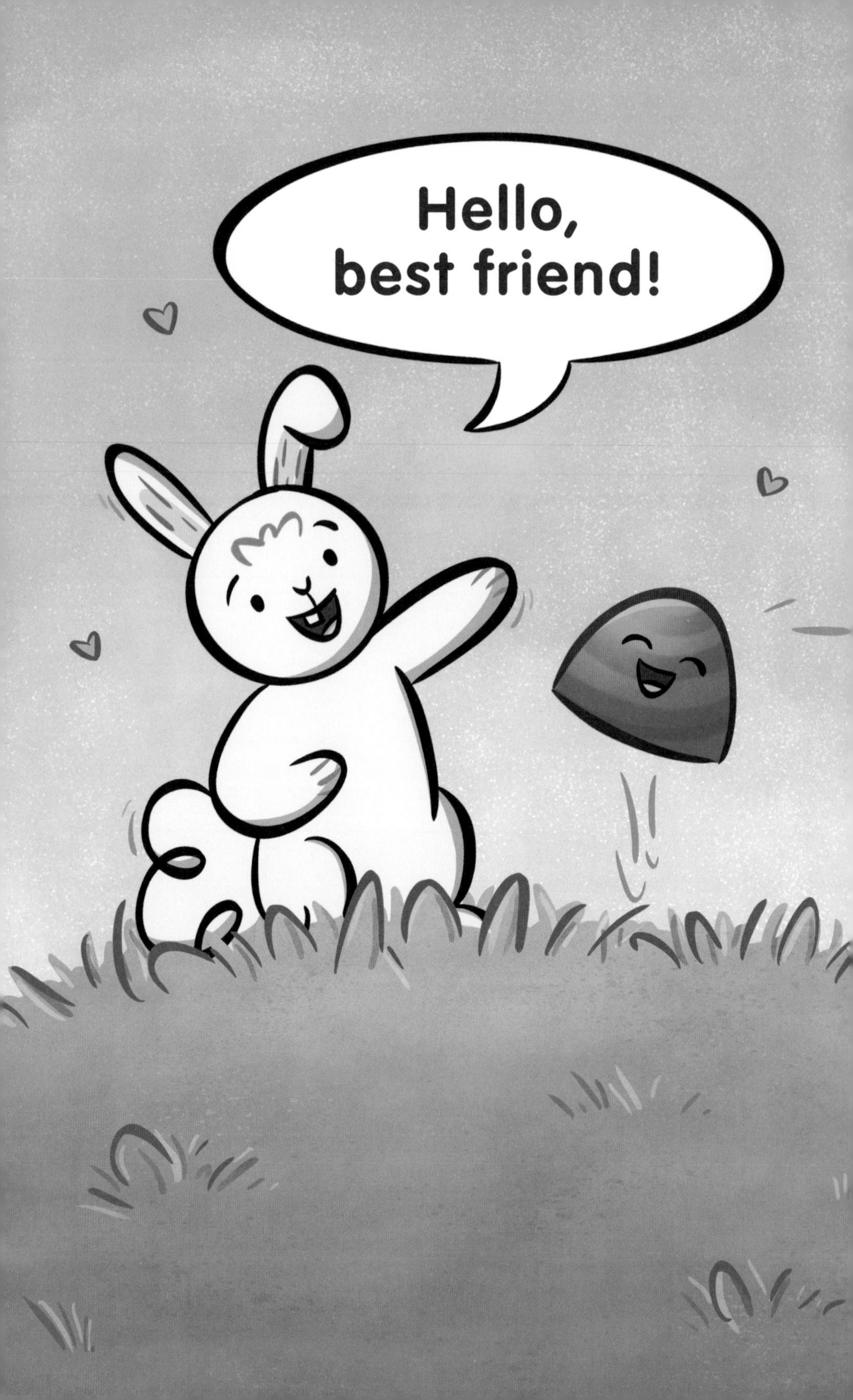
Hello,
best friend!

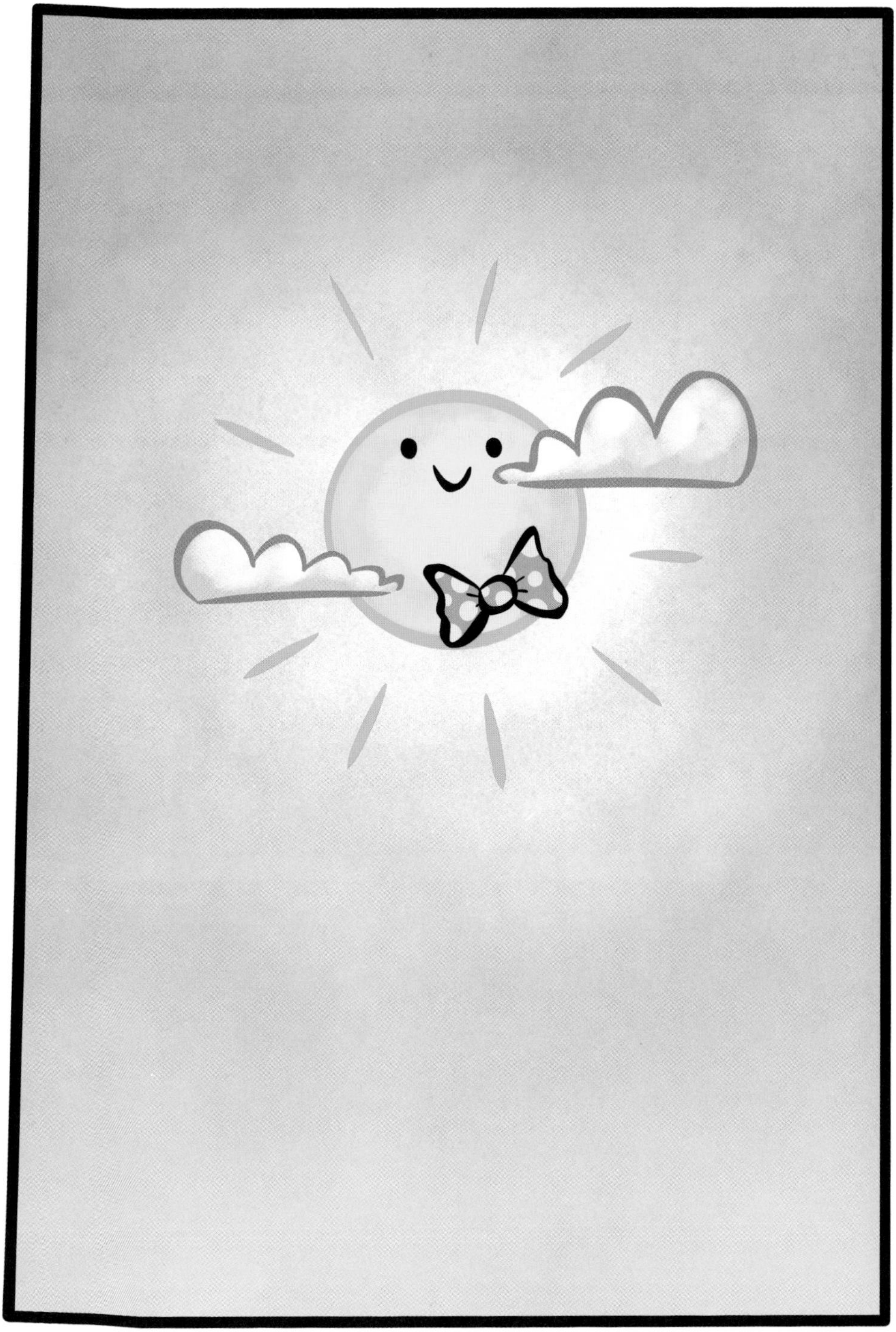

**JESS KEATING** is an award-winning author, cartoonist, and zoologist. She is the creator of over a dozen fiction and nonfiction books, including *Eat Your Rocks, Croc!*, *Shark Lady*, *Pink Is for Blobfish*, and the Elements of Genius middle-grade series. She lives in Ontario, Canada, where she's surrounded by books, bunnies, and bonbons. To learn more, tweet her @Jess_Keating, or visit jesskeating.com, where she shares behind-the-scenes work, resources for kids, and her daily writer's notebook of creative curiosities.